# HAPPY HOLIDAYS, JESSI

*Caryn Pearson*

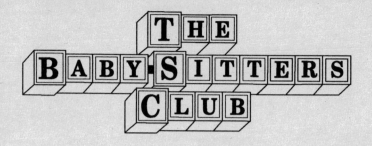

# HAPPY HOLIDAYS, JESSI

# Ann M. Martin

AN
**APPLE**
PAPERBACK

SCHOLASTIC INC.
New York Toronto London Auckland Sydney

ISBN 0-590-69209-7

12 11 10 9 8 7 6 5 4 3 2 1          6 7 8 9/9 0 1/0

Printed in the U.S.A.                                    40

First Scholastic printing, December 1996

*The author gratefully acknowledges*
*Peter Lerangis*
*for his help in*
*preparing this manuscript.*

# CHAPTER 1

"*B*rrrrup!*" burped my little brother, John Philip, otherwise known as Squirt.

As my mom lifted him out of his high chair, he clapped his hands proudly and said, "Bup!"

"John Philip!" scolded my aunt Cecelia. "What do we say?"

"He can't talk yet, Aunt Cecelia!" shouted my sister, Becca, from the family room.

My dad stopped sweeping the kitchen floor and kissed the top of Squirt's head. "But he makes great sound effects."

"Yeeaaaa! Bup!" Squirt screamed, running into the living room.

Aunt Cecelia hurried after him. "Don't go in there before I've washed your hands!"

"O-o-o-oh, you better watch out, you better not cry . . . " a voice sang out from our living room CD player.

"You better not *bup*, I'm telling you why,"

1

sang Daddy, dancing with the broom. "Cecelia is hot onnnnn your tail!"

My mom, who was handing me dirty dishes from the kitchen table, burst out laughing.

Welcome to the Ramsey family of Stoney-brook, Connecticut. We're only six in number — Daddy, Mama, Aunt Cecelia, Becca, Squirt, and me (Jessi) — but we make the noise of a hundred. Sometimes Daddy calls us the Circus Ramseycus.

From the living room, Aunt Cecelia called out, "I'll be in there to see how clean those dishes are in a minute!"

Daddy rolled his eyes.

Daddy loves to tease Aunt Cecelia, and she likes to scold him. They've been like that all their lives. They're brother and sister, but you'd never believe it from looking at them. Daddy kind of reminds me of a prince in a fairy tale. He's tall and handsome, with a great sense of humor and a beautiful, deep voice. Aunt Cecelia's not naturally thin. She has a scratchy voice and she hardly ever cracks a smile. In a fairy tale, she'd probably be the witch. I love her dearly, but she can be hard to live with.

Aunt Cecelia claims she's younger than Daddy, but the only one who believes her is my little sister. (Becca's eight years old, so

2

she's easily fooled.) I, Jessica Ramsey, am eleven, which is old enough to smell a fib.

"He sees you when you're sweeping," Daddy sang as he swept. "And buys you a new car . . . "

"Daaaaaddyyyy!" Becca yelled.

Mama sighed. "For your father, life is 'Showtime at the Apollo.' "

"I'd give him the hook!" Aunt Cecelia called out.

Daddy jutted out his jaw. "You all don't respect real talent."

Crazy. What can I say?

Well, we had an excuse for acting so silly. It was the first of December. The beginning of the absolute best month of the year.

I don't know about you, but I think the holidays are truly magical. The moment I see the first Christmas decorations in the store windows, I'm a little kid again. I feed Christmas carol recordings into the CD player all day long. Thinking about presents, I'm weak in the knees. And when I look forward to a whole week of Kwanzaa, my eyes water. Honest.

The entire month of December I'm one big tingle.

"Yvonne called today," Mama said to Daddy. "She was wondering what our plans were for the holidays."

I nearly dropped a plate. Yvonne is my aunt. Her daughter, Keisha, is my all-time favorite cousin. We grew up together in Oakley, New Jersey, before my branch of the family moved to Stoneybrook. "Can they come over for Christmas?" I asked.

"Yeaaaaaa!" Becca shouted from the family room.

"Well, they're spending Christmas at home," Mama replied, "but they'd love to get together for Kwanzaa — "

"Can they?" I asked. "Oh, please please please please?"

Becca rushed in, clutching an enormous department store catalog. *"Pleeeeeeeease?"*

Daddy laughed. "As long as they bring some pecan pie, they're welcome in this house."

"Then we just have to figure out exactly when," Mama said.

"You're not planning to have them over for the entire week?" Aunt Cecelia called out from the bathroom. "That's an awful lot of work."

"Oh, Cecelia, don't be a Kwanzaa Grinch," Daddy said.

"Bup! Bup! Bup!" shouted Squirt, hopping into the kitchen.

"Could one of you change his diaper?" Aunt Cecelia said wearily. "I have got to clean my bedroom."

Daddy went running after Squirt. "Maybe

not a week," he said over his shoulder. "But a couple of days, at least."

"Definitely for the *karamu* feast," Mama agreed.

"Yeaaa!" I did a little pirouette in front of the dishwasher. Liquid flung outward from the coffee mug I was holding.

"Ewwwww!" Becca cried out. "Germs!"

"Jessi!" Mama warned.

"Oops. Sorry!"

I couldn't help it. I was ecstatic. And when I'm ecstatic, I dance.

Even when I'm just plain happy, I dance.

Actually, I dance when I'm depressed, too. And when I'm feeling medium-okay.

That's one thing you should know about me. I'm basically a dance maniac. I *jeté* from class to class in the halls of Stoneybrook Middle School. I practice walking *en pointe* in my yard when I'm mowing the lawn in the summer. At meetings of the Baby-sitters Club (a group I belong to), I do stretches and practice *pliés*.

If you already know that a *jeté* is a leap, *en pointe* means "on the point of the toe," and *pliés* are knee bends, then you're probably a balletomane like me. (If you're not, I need to explain that "balletomane" means "ballet freak.") I take ballet class in Stamford, Connecticut, which is the city closest to Stoneybrook. My number one goal in life is to be a ballerina (preferably famous, but that's not required).

As I loaded up more plates, I heard Aunt Cecelia call from her bedroom, "Don't worry about the dishes! I'll be there in a minute to help — and whatever I can't do, we'll do in the morning!"

Daddy came back in, holding Squirt. "Translation?" he whispered. "Do it now, or you'll be scraping dried, crusty collard greens off those plates before breakfast."

*"Brother John, I heard that!"* boomed Aunt Cecelia's voice.

Daddy pursed his lips into an exaggerated *Ooooo*, like a little boy who's been caught. Then he raced upstairs with Squirt.

Becca was now sitting at the kitchen table, using a thick red marker to circle something in the catalog. "I want this, too!"

"Making your list for Santa?" Mama asked.

"Yeah, right." Becca rolled her eyes. "Like I believe in him? I'm not a *baby*."

"You told me you were going to mail that to the North Pole," I reminded her.

"That's, like, just in case," Becca said. "I mean, maybe there's no reindeer and stuff, but a factory that he runs — you know, with Ex-Lax or something."

Mama burst out laughing. "I think you mean Fed Ex."

"Whatever," Becca said, circling a new bike. "If I mail this tomorrow, will it get there in time for Christmas?"

"Twenty-four days? Sure," Mama said.

*Twenty-four.* That meant only twenty-five until Kwanzaa, thirty-one until the New Year.

I rose *en pointe*. I did a perfect arabesque against the dishwasher and dumped in a load of dirty silverware.

I thought about a Christmas tree. The smell of logs in the fireplace. Exchanging gifts with my best friends in the Baby-sitters Club. Making Kwanzaa stuff with Keisha and her little brother, Billy.

Do you know about Kwanzaa? You probably do if you're African-American, like us Ramseys. If you don't, I'll tell you.

It's the coolest holiday. It lasts seven whole days. The entire family participates, with lots of crafts-making, feasts, gift-giving, visiting, and storytelling.

Kwanzaa was conceived of in 1966 by an African-American professor named Dr. Maulana Karenga. He had seen a neighborhood in Los Angeles destroyed by race riots. He wanted to create a special celebration to unify the African-American community.

Dr. Karenga studied the rituals of many different African tribes. He discovered that a lot of celebrations take place around the winter harvest season. He took different parts of each ritual and combined them, creating a holiday that was modern and meaningful.

"Kwanza" means "first" in Swahili. Why first? Because it's a time when we African-Americans put our people and our families first. Also, the holiday ends on the first of the new year. And the African rituals celebrate the first fruits of the harvest.

Dr. Karenga wanted the holiday name to have seven letters, one for each of the days. "Kwanza" has six. So which letter did he add? *A*. The first letter of the alphabet!

Each day has a special theme. The first is *umoja*, or togetherness. The theme: "We help each other."

The second day is *kujichagulia*, or self-determination: "We decide things for ourselves."

The third is *ujima*, or collective work and responsibility: "We work together to make life better."

*Ujamaa*, or cooperative economics, is the fourth: "We build and support our businesses."

The fifth day is about *nia*, or purpose: "We have a reason for living."

8

My personal favorite is the sixth day, *kuumba*, or creativity: "We use our minds and hands to make things." On that night, we have a big feast to celebrate the end of the holiday.

On the last day (*imani*, or faith), we relax and think about the nicest theme of all: "We believe in ourselves, our ancestors, and our future."

"Done!" I said, closing the dishwasher.

The table was spotless. Mama was reading a magazine, sitting across from Becca.

Daddy walked in, holding Squirt. "All clean!" he said.

"Keeeeeen," Squirt echoed.

"Who wants hot cocoa with marshmallows?" Daddy announced.

"Meeeeee!" Mama, Becca, and I answered.

As Daddy headed for the stove, I heard a familiar creaking of the floorboards. Aunt Cecelia peered into the kitchen.

I could see that Daddy looked proud of our work. "Come on in, Cecelia," he said. "The dishes are clean. We're having cocoa. You're just in time."

"You're taking a break?" Aunt Cecelia huffed as she sponged off the counter.

"Marshmallows for me!" Becca said.

"Me, too," I added.

"None for me," Mama said.

"Doos!" added Squirt (which means *juice*).

Aunt Cecelia settled herself in her seat and cleared her throat. "Well, I suppose some cocoa would settle my stomach," she said. "No marshmallows, but I could go for a little of that vanilla ice cream . . . "

"All riiiiight, Aunt Cecelia!" I said.

What a life. A peaceful Sunday night. The hint of snow in the air. A nice, quiet family evening over hot cocoa. Just perfect.

As Daddy opened the freezer, Aunt Cecelia said, "The low-fat variety, please! And, oh my lord, will someone turn down the heat under the pot? Honestly, John, don't you know you're not supposed to boil the milk?"

Well, almost perfect, anyway.

## CHAPTER 2

"It's spitting," said Claudia Kishi, gazing upward through her bedroom window.

"Is it white, fluffy spit?" asked Mallory Pike. "Or clear?"

"It's spit spit," answered Abby Stevenson.

"Isn't it too cold for spit spit?" Mary Anne Spier remarked.

"Uh, I hate to interrupt," Kristy Thomas announced, "but I call this meeting of the Baby-spitters — *sitters* — Club to order!"

Claudia and Mary Anne sat back on Claudia's bed. Abby plunked down on the carpet, next to Mallory and me. Stacey McGill sat on Claudia's desk chair.

Kristy, as usual, was sitting on a director's chair, wearing her visor and keeping her eye on the clock. (Kristy is the Baby-sitters Club president, and she would never, ever allow a meeting to start late.)

We were all in our places, ready to begin.

Well, our bodies were. Our minds were outside in the spit.

The weather report had said it might snow. It was only December second, so no one really believed it. But in New England, you never know. The stuff outside seemed too wet for snow but too light for rain.

"I think it's sleet," Claudia said.

"What's the difference between freezing rain and sleet?" Stacey asked.

Mary Anne frowned. "They're the same thing, aren't they?"

"No," Kristy declared. "Sleet is, you know, rain that's ice. Freezing rain is . . . uh, well, it's . . . "

"Ice that's rain?" Claudia asked.

"That's it!" Kristy replied. "Or whatever."

Abby giggled. "Thank you, Professor."

"I'll ask my sister." Claudia sprang off the bed, opened her door, and called down the hall: "Ja-*niiiiiine!*"

"Who-o-oa!" Kristy said. "Come on, guys. It's Monday. First things first!"

"Dues!" Stacey chimed in. She pulled out a ragged manila envelope from under the bed and held it open.

We all rummaged in our pockets, grumbling and moaning.

Yes, we pay dues. The Baby-sitters Club is a serious business. We meet three days a week,

Mondays, Wednesdays, and Fridays, from 5:30 to 6:00. We have officers, rules, a record book, an official notebook (a journal of our job experiences), and a ton of regular clients.

How did we get so organized? Two words: Kristy Thomas. She invented the BSC. It happened one evening when she saw her mom calling all over town to find a baby-sitter for Kristy's little brother, David Michael.

Back then, Kristy lived in a small house across the street from Claudia. Her dad had abandoned the family a few years earlier. So Mrs. Thomas had to rely on Kristy and her two older brothers, Charlie and Sam, to do a lot of sitting. Well, they were all busy that evening. And poor Mrs. Thomas could not find one sitter in the whole town.

Kristy to the rescue. She knew what Stoneybrook needed: an agency for sitters — one central phone number, satisfaction guaranteed.

So she created it.

The first club members were Kristy, Mary Anne, Claudia, and Stacey. But they became so popular that they had to add new members (such as *moi*). Now we have ten members altogether, including two associates and an honorary member who lives in California. We all keep each other up-to-date about the various changes in the lives of our clients' kids by writing about them in the BSC notebook.

Mallory Pike and I are the youngest sitters. We're both eleven and in sixth grade. All the other BSC members are thirteen-year-old eighth-graders. Well, except for Claudia. I'll explain about that later.

The BSC has had its ups and downs. Not long ago, we even split up for awhile. We were getting on each other's nerves and were tired of all the work. But don't worry, the split-up didn't last long. These days we're stronger than ever.

President Kristy runs the meetings and basically bosses everybody around. But we respect her a lot. She is the Kid Expert. Honestly, she can figure out how to make any kid happy. When several of our younger charges complained that they wanted to play softball but couldn't find a team to join — *voilà!* Kristy organized them into a team called Kristy's Krushers. Another great Kristy idea was Kid-Kits — boxes filled with games, toys, and knickknacks. We take them on our jobs, and kids think they're incredibly cool.

Kristy's very forceful. I think she'd scare me if I weren't taller than she is. (Despite our age difference, she's only five feet tall and I'm five-two.) Kristy has brown eyes and brown hair, which is usually pulled back into a ponytail. She wears old, casual, comfortable clothes all the time, even though her family's super rich.

You see, the Thomases no longer live in that house near Claudia. Kristy's mom got remarried, to this millionaire named Watson Brewer. He lived in a mansion and had two children from a previous marriage (Karen and Andrew, who live with him every other month). So Kristy gained a nice new dad, a humongous home on the other side of Stoneybrook, and two new siblings. Then Kristy's parents adopted a two-year-old Vietnamese girl and named her Emily. After the adoption, Kristy's grandmother, Nannie, moved in to help take care of Emily. Add in Kristy's brothers and a lot of pets, and that big old house can seem like a crowded train station.

Kristy's best friend in the BSC is Mary Anne Spier. She looks a little like Kristy, but her hair is shorter, she wears preppy-ish clothes, and she has the exact opposite personality. Mary Anne is quiet, shy, and sensitive. She is the best listener and the most loyal friend. And it doesn't take much to make her cry.

Actually, even *I* cry when I think about Mary Anne's life. Her mom died when she was a baby. Mr. Spier was so grief-stricken that he had to let Mary Anne's grandparents raise her for a while. Then, when he was ready to take Mary Anne back, they said no way. They believed that being a single parent would be too hard for him. Well, Mr. Spier did get Mary Anne back, but as she grew up, he went overboard on parenting. He raised Mary Anne super strictly — early curfews, a very conservative dress code, little-girl hairstyles. It wasn't until Mary Anne was in seventh grade that he started to loosen up.

Now, here's the really teary part. One day, a girl named Dawn Schafer joined the BSC. She had been born and raised in California, but her parents had divorced. Mrs. Schafer was a Stoneybrook native, so she decided to move back here with Dawn and Dawn's younger brother, Jeff. Well, guess who her high school sweetheart had been?

Mary Anne's dad!

They had been seriously in LUV, but Dawn's grandmother had disapproved of the relationship. BUT — deeee-deee-deeeee (those are romantic violins) — years later, the love was still there! They were married (sigh). So Mary Anne and her dad moved into the Schafers' funky, two-hundred-year-old farmhouse. (I wish I could say the story has a perfect ending, but it doesn't. First Jeff grew miserably homesick and moved back with his dad, and then Dawn did, too. She's the honorary BSC member I told you about.)

16

Fortunately, Dawn visits a lot. And Mary Anne talks to her on the phone all the time. But I know Mary Anne misses her awfully. (Boy, do I understand. When we moved from Oakley, I thought my heart would break from missing Keisha.)

Mary Anne may be emotional, but when it comes to her BSC job, she's steady as a rock. As secretary, she handles the official record book. It includes our job calendar; a list of client names, addresses, and rates; and special information about our charges. Mary Anne manages to keep all that stuff up-to-date. On the calendar, she carefully records all our conflicts — doctor appointments, after-school activities, and family obligations. When a client calls, we take down the information about the sitting job and promise to call back. Then Mary Anne checks the calendar. She tells us who's available and tries to distribute jobs evenly. Just between you and me, I'd go crazy if I had her job. But to Mary Anne, it's fun. If Kristy has a Big Idea Mind, Mary Anne has an Organization Mind.

Stacey, on the other hand, has a Math Mind. That's why she's club treasurer. She collects dues and keeps track of our "treasury." At the end of each month she pays Claudia for her phone bill and gives Charlie Thomas gas money (he drives Abby and Kristy to our meetings). Whatever's left over buys Kid-Kit supplies. If we're really lucky, we have enough for a pizza party or a special event for our charges.

You would recognize Stacey instantly at a meeting. She's the blonde girl dressed like a *Vogue* model. I adore her clothes. Lots of black, sleek and urban. Very New York City. Which makes sense, because she grew up in Manhattan, until seventh grade. Then she moved to Stoneybrook. Twice. The first time was with her mom and dad, when Mr. McGill's company transferred him to Connecticut. Not long after, he was transferred back to N.Y.C. Unfortunately, the McGills' marriage wasn't doing well, and all the moving made it worse. They divorced, and Stacey chose to move back to Stoneybrook with her mom.

Stacey visits her dad a lot. Each time she goes, she has to remember to pack a special kit for insulin injections. You see, she has diabetes. When she eats sugar, it goes straight to her bloodstream. That's because her pancreas doesn't produce this hormone called insulin, which parcels sugar into the blood a little at a time. Eating a candy bar at the wrong time could make Stacey seriously ill. But fortunately diabetes is controllable. Stacey just needs to take her medicine daily (she insists the injections aren't as gross as they sound), stay away from refined sugar, and eat meals on a strict schedule.

What's the opposite of a diabetic? Claudia Kishi. She thrives on refined sugar. If she gave up candy, I think she'd shrivel away. Her room is like a junk food minefield — candy bars between folded shirts, bags of chips in shoe boxes, bags of pretzels wedged between her piles of art supplies. If nonmelting ice cream were invented, she'd insulate her walls with it. Why does she hide all this stuff? Because if her parents knew, they'd pass out. They're anti-bad nutrition. (Also anti-pop culture. Claudia has to hide her Nancy Drew books.)

Claudia is nothing like the rest of her family. Mr. Kishi has some important job in high finance, Mrs. Kishi is a librarian, and Janine is a high school kid with a genius IQ who takes college courses. Claud's a free spirit. She's funny. She can't spell to save her life. Her grades were so bad she had to repeat seventh grade. She has long, silky black hair and dresses in crazy styles. And she is the most talented artist you have ever seen. Painting, sculpting, drawing, jewelry making — Claudia does it all.

For a long time, Claudia felt like an alien in her super-intellectual family. Only her grandmother, Mimi, understood her. Mimi lived with the Kishis. Although her English wasn't great (she was born and raised in Japan, like all of Claudia's grandparents), she and Claudia learned to communicate beautifully. When Mimi died, Claudia was devastated. She keeps a photo of Mimi on her wall for inspiration.

Claudia's our vice-president. She hosts all the meetings, feeds us junk food, and answers phone calls that stray in during off hours.

"Sleet is falling ice," explained Janine, leaning against Claudia's door. "Freezing rain is water. It only becomes ice when it hits frozen ground."

With that, she went back to her room. We heard the clacking of computer keys.

"Wow," Abby said. "She's like a walking CD-ROM. Can I rent her?"

Abby is our newest member. She cracks me up. The thing is, she doesn't try to be funny; she just is. She's like that with sports, too: a fabulous athlete without working hard at it. (Kristy is very jealous of that, but she'd never admit it.) Abby's hair is this huge tangle of black curls. She has pearly skin and wears glasses or contact lenses. If you meet her, don't be surprised if she talks as if she has a cold. She's allergic to a million things. She also has asthma and always carries an inhaler with her.

To the BSC, Abby was like a gift that dropped from the sky. Actually, she rode in from Long Island. That's where she, her mom, and her twin sister, Anna, used to live (her dad died in a car accident when the girls were nine). They moved into a house on Kristy's block shortly after Dawn left for California.

We invited both Stevenson girls to join, but Anna declined. She's a gifted violinist, and she practices for hours every day. Anna is kind of quiet and serious. (The only time I've seen Abby like that was when the twins had their Bat Mitzvah. That's a religious rite for thirteen-year-old Jewish girls. Abby and Anna both read from the Torah, the first five books of the Bible, written in Hebrew.)

Abby's our alternate officer, which means she takes over for any absent officer.

Our associate members, Shannon Kilbourne and Logan Bruno, help us out whenever we have an overflow of jobs. They're not required to attend meetings or pay dues. Shannon goes to a private school called Stoneybrook Day School, where she's involved in lots of after-school stuff. Logan is Mary Anne's boyfriend. He's on just about every sports team, so he's always at practices.

Of course, I'm saving the best for last. The youngest but most valuable members — Mallory and me! We're called junior officers, but don't let that fool you. We give full baby-sitter value. The only thing we can't do is take late sitting jobs on weekdays. Why? Because our parents treat us like babies, that's why.

Next to Keisha, Mallory is my best friend in the world. She's the only girl I've ever met who adores reading horse books as much as I do. Like me, Mal is the oldest kid in her family. But her family is enormous — seven younger brothers and sisters! And that includes ten-year-old triplet brothers. Can you imagine?

Mallory has thick, reddish-brown hair and light, freckled skin. She wears braces and glasses. She begged her parents to let her wear contacts, but they said she couldn't until she is fifteen. (I told you our parents treat us like babies.)

*Riiiinng!*

At 5:40 our first call came in. Abby snatched up the receiver. "Hello, the all-weather Babysitters Club! We sit in the sleet, we sit in the freezing rain . . . " Abby's face suddenly turned red. "Uh, well, no, Mrs. Harris, we don't actually *sit* in the rain. I meant *baby*-sit. You know . . . uh-huh . . . yes. . . . Okay, I'll call you back."

Abby hung up and buried her face in her hands. "Duhhh, me and my big mouth."

We were howling with laughter.

"Ahem," Abby said. "A family named the

Harrises needs someone to baby-sit for their boys a week from Thursday."

"Yyyyes!" Kristy said. "New clients! How did they find out about us?"

Abby shrugged. "How should I know?"

The name sounded familiar. "Are the boys' names Omar and Ebon?" I asked.

"Yeah," Abby replied.

"They're cute," I went on. "My mom and I met them at the supermarket. They were already Kwanzaa shopping."

Mary Anne looked up from the record book. "You're busy that day, Jessi. But I could do it."

Kristy looked agitated about something. "So I guess they're, like, African-American?"

"Yeah," I replied.

"I mean, because of Kwanzaa and all, I just assumed . . . "

"Uh-huh, so?"

"Nothing." Kristy looked out the window.

I felt a little creepy. I mean, my BSC friends are not bigots. But that reaction was weird.

"Nothing?" I asked. "Or something you don't want to tell me?"

Kristy shrugged. "Well, does it ever bother you . . . you know, Kwanzaa being only for one race of people?"

I shrugged. "No."

"I mean, I don't mean to sound like a jerk,

but isn't that kind of biased? Excluding people on the basis of skin color?"

Stacey was shaking her head. "I don't believe I'm hearing this."

"Well, African-Americans can celebrate Christmas, right?" Kristy countered. "Everybody can."

Abby raised her hand. "Uh, hello? Not *everybody*."

"Kristy," I said, "Hanukkah is a holiday for Jewish people. Kwanzaa's a holiday for African-Americans. Lots of nationalities and cultures have their own holidays."

"The Papadakises celebrate name days," Mary Anne spoke up. "One for each person. It's like having another birthday."

"The Greeks aren't *excluding* anyone," I continued. "Neither are the Jews. They're doing something positive. Following a tradition that's meaningful to them."

Kristy nodded. "Makes sense. I guess I don't really know anything about Kwanzaa."

"Not too many people do," I said.

What I really meant to say was *white* people. Which made me think. Why don't they know about Kwanzaa?

Answer: It's a quiet, family holiday. And in Stoneybrook, there aren't many African-American families.

Okay, fine. But why not spread the word?

My mom always says people are afraid of stuff they don't know. If Kristy could think Kwanzaa was a racist idea, maybe other people could, too. They'd never know all the wonderful aspects. They'd never know the feeling of pride and togetherness Kwanzaa brings.

And they *should* know.

"Maybe Stamford has a Kwanzaa festival we could go to," Abby said.

"Why don't we have one here in Stoneybrook?" I suggested.

"Great idea!" Abby exclaimed.

"I was just about to suggest the same thing," Kristy mumbled.

The idea was taking shape in my mind. "It would be fun — families eating great food, kids displaying Kwanzaa crafts . . . "

"African folktales," Mallory chimed in.

"An artistic display about the history of Africa," Claudia added.

"Or about the seven principles of Kwanzaa," I said.

"Huh?" Abby asked.

I went through the description, day by day. I knew my friends were hooked.

Somehow or other, I, Jessi Ramsey, was going to organize the first annual Stoneybrook Kwanzaa festival.

# CHAPTER 3

"*So I called up the Stoneybrook Community Center, and guess who answered the phone?*"

I practically had to shout my question to Becca. I was in the front seat of Aunt Cecelia's noisy old Volkswagen. We were on our way to a department store called Bellair's to do holiday shopping.

Becca leaned forward in the backseat. "What did you say?"

*Honk! Honnnnnnnk!*

Aunt Cecelia was blaring her horn. "And where did *you* get your driver's license?" she shouted, glaring straight ahead. "The five and dime?"

I snapped around and looked out the windshield. A car was entering the lane far in front of us, its signals flashing.

"Mercy, will you look at these maniacs on the road!" Aunt Cecelia grumbled. "They think this is a racetrack!"

Becca was peering out the window. "I don't see any maniacs."

To be honest, I didn't either. All I saw were cars whizzing by us on the right at normal speeds. Aunt Cecelia was puttering along slo-o-o-owly in the left lane of the highway.

"Isn't the left lane for passing?" I asked. "Maybe if you drove in the center — "

"*Please*, Jessica!" Aunt Cecelia cut me off. "When you have your license, I will listen to your suggestions."

"Peeeeez, Decca!" Squirt echoed from his car seat behind me.

I turned and tickled Squirt. Then I continued shouting to Becca: *"When I called the Community Center, Ms. Lebeque answered! Remember, the woman who was in charge of the summer day camp, where I was a junior counselor?"*

"Uh-huh!" Becca replied.

*"Anyway, I asked her about the Kwanzaa festival, and she spoke to the head of the center, and guess what? We can have it there in the gym, on New Year's Eve!"*

Becca bounced up and down on her seat. *"Yeeaaa!"*

Next to her, Squirt squealed with happiness. *"Aaaaay!"*

Out of the corner of my eye, I spotted a minivan driving onto the highway. It slid comfortably into the lane next to ours.

*Honnnnnnk!* We all lurched forward as Aunt Cecelia clomped down on the brake.

"Hush!" she shouted. "I can't concentrate with you screaming. That man nearly killed us!"

"He did not," I said.

*"Slow down! Where's the fire?"* Aunt Cecelia thundered. "Honestly, that young man has children in the car!"

"He can't hear you, Aunt Cecelia!" Becca said, giggling.

"You see, Jessica, you set the example!" Aunt Cecelia retorted. "When you back talk, your sister follows. You'll be having your brother at it next."

I tried to turn toward Becca, but my stomach was knotting up and I started feeling nauseous. Let me tell you, a ride with Aunt Cecelia is like a day on a roller coaster.

By the time we reached the Bellair's parking lot, I thought I was going to puke.

Aunt Cecelia passed a lot of empty spaces in the back of the lot. She drove close to the entrance, where the cars were packed tight.

Slowly, she inched right into a space marked for the handicapped.

"Aunt Cecelia, you're not supposed to park here," I said as gently as I could.

"Jessica Ramsey, do you see any other spaces?" Aunt Cecelia asked.

"In the back — "

"Darling, I have three children and an arthritic ankle," Aunt Cecelia replied. "Besides, there are other empty handicapped spots. That means the police will not ticket."

Daddy has a phrase for an argument like that. Cecelian Logic. He says no one can understand it but Aunt Cecelia.

I climbed out of the car and pushed the front seat forward. Then I reached into the back, unhooked Squirt's car seat harness, and helped him out.

"Anyway," I said to Becca as we both guided him into a collapsible stroller we'd brought along, "I'm trying to figure out what should be in the festival. You know that elevated area at the end of the big conference room? We could use it as a stage, for a skit."

"Starring Becca Ramsey," Becca said, gently hooking Squirt's stroller straps.

"We'll see," I said with a laugh. "But we have to talk this up, okay? I want Omar and Ebon Harris involved, Sara Ford, Bob Ingram, whoever."

Aunt Cecelia let out a little sarcastic snort. "And who do you expect is going to take care of all the preparations?"

"My friends in the BSC will help out," I replied, holding open the front door of Bellair's.

Aunt Cecelia pushed the stroller past me. "Jessica, come down from your cloud. Do you realize how much we grown-ups have to do around the holidays? What do you think is going to happen when eight-year-olds are bothering their mommies and daddies about cooking up food and making place mats . . . "

She walked straight into the store, scolding away. Becca ran alongside the stroller and began tickling Squirt. He screamed with pleasure.

"Don't get him too excited," Aunt Cecelia warned her. "He won't nap."

I stopped at a display of gorgeous carved-wood jewelry. "Oooooh, look," I called out. "I would love these."

"Cool!" Becca shouted.

"Tool!" Squirt echoed.

"Girls, we are shopping for *others*," Aunt Cecelia reprimanded us.

"Well, if you just happened to be thinking of what to buy me for Christmas," I teased, "you might wander over here while my back is turned . . . "

Aunt Cecelia shook her head. "You know, your daddy and I couldn't tell our parents what to buy us for Christmas. We were grateful for whatever we received, no matter how humble. We respected our parents' hard work, and we knew they'd do the best they could . . . "

Out of sight of Aunt Cecelia, Becca inserted two fingers into her mouth and pretended to barf.

I stifled a giggle. "Where did you learn that?"

"From you," Becca replied.

" . . . one present each," Aunt Cecelia droned on. "And that was in the good years. And you never saw us complain . . . "

"Men's shirts!" Becca exclaimed, pointing to a distant sign. "That's what Daddy needs."

"Shirts are expensive," Aunt Cecelia said. "Come with me to accessories. You'll find something more reasonable."

Shopping is a funny thing. With friends, it's great. With grown-ups, it can be incredibly boring.

With Aunt Cecelia, it's a little like torture.

Becca and I were determined to buy a shirt. But we obediently followed Aunt Cecelia into men's accessories. There she argued with a sales clerk over the price of a pair of wool socks.

In ladies' lingerie, Aunt Cecelia looked at some bras for about an hour. She waved off two clerks who offered help. Two minutes later she stormed away, complaining that no one was assisting her.

Squirt fell asleep while we were in kitchen appliances. I don't blame him. Aunt Cecelia was raising a ruckus with the manager because her favorite type of blender was now made out of plastic instead of glass. Or something like that.

Becca and I were struggling to keep our eyes open. So far, we hadn't gone to any of the departments *we* needed to go to.

"This is so boring," Becca complained.

I was gazing through a Plexiglas barrier into the section next to us. I could see a rack labeled "Jokes 'n' Notions" near a huge sign that said PARTY GOODS.

Aunt Cecelia and the manager were still fussing. Squirt was out cold, making little baby-snores.

I pulled Becca by the sleeve. "We'll be right back," I called out to Aunt Cecelia's back.

We ran around the Plexiglas divider into the party goods area.

"Yuck!" Becca said, pulling a plastic bloody eye out of a bin.

I found a rubbery tarantula and shook it so that it quivered. *"Aaahh, it's alive!"*

Becca screamed.

I looked through the Plexiglas. Now Aunt Cecelia was yelling at two managers. Both of them were nodding like animated dolls.

I strapped on a fake Santa beard and a plastic pig snout. Becca donned a pair of glasses with a mustache and a hat of foam plastic that looked as if an axe were embedded in it.

We were howling.

Then I caught a glimpse of two sales clerks looking at us. They were giggling, too.

"Let's scare Aunt Cecelia," Becca said behind her mustache.

"She's in a sour mood," I said.

"She always is! This will make her laugh."

Becca walked around the Plexiglas barrier. She crouched behind a stack of food processors a few feet away from Aunt Cecelia.

I followed. Through a gap between the boxes we could see one of the managers hanging up the phone and smiling weakly at Aunt Cecelia. "You're in luck, ma'am," he said. "The factory has a few of the old model in storage, and they'll send one to us right away."

"Of course they will. I'll be back." Without a good-bye, Aunt Cecelia turned and pushed the stroller in our direction. "Jessica? Rebecca?"

I put my hand on Becca's shoulder. Just a few more steps and Aunt Cecelia would be in the perfect place, right in front of us.

". . . no sense of discipline whatsoever . . . " Her voice was coming closer. "I don't know why I bother to — "

*Now.*

"Boooo!"

"*Oh!*" Aunt Cecelia put her hand over her chest and staggered backward. "Oh, mercy! Oh!"

Becca burst into giggles. "Surprise!"

Squirt awoke with a start. "Eeeee!" he cried, twisting under his strap.

For a moment Aunt Cecelia didn't say a word. She glowered at Becca, then at me, her lips pursed tightly.

I knew that look. We were dead meat.

"Follow me," Aunt Cecelia snapped, pushing the stroller toward the exit. "We are leaving."

I pulled off my disguise. "Why?"

"Sorryyyyy," Becca pleaded.

"Eeeeeee!" Squirt screamed.

"And you better return that merchandise!" Aunt Cecelia called over her shoulder.

Becca and I ran back to the party section. We dumped our disguises and followed Aunt Cecelia.

"But we didn't buy anything!" Becca protested.

Aunt Cecelia stared straight ahead without replying.

"Please, Aunt Cecelia?" I begged.

Aunt Cecelia marched forward like a wooden soldier. Squirt was squalling, probably wet and hungry. Becca began crying.

As we charged through the exit, a Salvation Army Santa was ringing a bell. "Ho ho ho!" he boomed. "Merry Christmas!"

Aunt Cecelia ignored him. She went straight to the car.

But just before we reached it, she stopped in her tracks and gasped, "Well, of all the nerve . . . "

Neatly folded under the windshield wiper was a white parking ticket.

I wanted to say "I told you so," but I kept my mouth shut.

Sometimes it's better to quit while you're behind.

# CHAPTER 4

"It's perfect!" Kristy said. "I mean, all the Kwanzaa principles are right there — "

Claudia was shaking her head. "No, Kristy."

"Unity . . . self-determination . . . " Kristy counted out the words on her fingers.

"The history of the Baby-sitters Club," Abby said, "is not the right topic for a Kwanzaa skit."

"Cooperative economics . . . " Kristy continued, "collective work and responsibility . . . purpose . . . Hey, those concepts *are* the BSC!"

We all stared at her, stunned.

"The kids could play themselves," Kristy barged on. "Think of the great publicity!"

"Kristyyyyy . . . " Mary Anne said warningly.

Claudia's clock clicked to five-thirty. "Well, we're off to a good start," Kristy said. "I call this meeting to order!"

"Chow time!" Claudia announced, pulling a bag of Cape Cod potato chips out of her pillowcase.

"Dues!" Stacey added.

We quickly paid up and grabbed some chips. Kristy was munching away, finally silent.

I reached into my backpack for a pile of Kwanzaa books I'd borrowed from the library. Mallory and I had gone there two days earlier, after the awful trip to Bellair's.

All weekend long we'd read up on Kwanzaa and African-American stories. That day at lunch we'd come up with a great idea for a skit.

"Jessi and I did some research," Mallory began.

"This book is great," I said, leafing through *Her Stories*, by Virginia Hamilton. "It's all folktales and stories about African-American women."

"Research for what?" Kristy asked.

"The play," Mal replied.

"But — but what about my idea?" Kristy sputtered.

"Save it for Hollywood," Abby suggested.

"Have some more chips, Kristy," Claudia said.

Kristy scowled and slumped into her chair.

"I was thinking of this story called 'Malindy and Little Devil.'" I found an illustration from it and held up the book. "It's about this farm girl who meets the devil on a road."

"But he's a *little* devil, " Mal continued, "doing his first devilment. He's never had a soul and he wants one desperately. So he makes Malindy promise to give him hers when she reaches womanhood."

"And she does," I added.

Total, baffled silence.

"That's it?" Stacey asked.

"At least the history of the BSC has a happy ending," Kristy grumbled.

"So does this," I continued. "See, when the devil finally comes to collect, Malindy hands him what he asked for. A sole . . . from her shoe!"

"Ohhhhhh," groaned Abby and Claudia.

"He doesn't know any better," Mallory said. "So he kind of scratches his head, *duhhh* — "

"And Malindy skips away, free as a bird," I concluded.

Stacey laughed out loud. "All riiight, Malindy."

"The kids will adore it," Mary Anne said with a smile.

"Some of the smaller or shyer kids can play

animals who live on Malindy's farm," I suggested.

Kristy was nodding her head slowly. "Not bad, but it's missing something . . . "

"How many kids have volunteered to be in this?" Abby asked.

"I'll find out when I talk to Becca," I replied.

Kristy blurted out, "I've got it! As a young woman, Malindy belongs to an organization of baby-sitters. The day she has to give her soul away, the sitters come up with the shoe idea at a meeting — "

"Attack!" Claudia grabbed a pillow and threw it at Kristy.

"What?" Kristy said, cowering. "What'd I say?"

*Rrrring!*

Claudia picked up the phone. "Hello, Baby-sitters Club!" she said sweetly.

Well, the phone hardly stopped ringing for the rest of the half hour. In between calls, we made plans.

We decided to set aside certain weekend days for festival rehearsals. Claudia volunteered to make fliers and posters. Kristy promised she'd force Charlie to drive her around into the surrounding towns, where she'd post fliers wherever she could. (You see, Kristy does have good ideas.)

After the meeting, I was flying. My little idea was going to come true. I *jetéd* all the way home.

"I'm ho-o-o-ome!" I sang as I opened the front door.

Hurricane Becca nearly knocked me over. *"They can do it they can do it!* All the kids want to be in the festival!"

"Yeaaaa!" I grabbed Becca and started dancing across the room.

We stopped when we ran smack into Aunt Cecelia at the kitchen door.

"Ahem," she said. "Do you girls expect the salad to make itself?"

I could see Mama and Daddy preparing dinner at the kitchen counter. "Hug time first!"

Becca and I ran into the family room to hug Squirt, who was in his playpen. Then I went back to the kitchen to help.

I told Mama and Daddy all about our plans. I mentioned the kids Becca had involved and described "Malindy and Little Devil."

They both thought the idea was fantastic. (I knew they would.)

I could hear Aunt Cecelia's orthopedic shoes click-clacking dully on the kitchen floor behind me. "And what does this story have to do with Kwanzaa?" she asked.

"Well, I guess you could say it's about self-determination," I replied.

"Creativity," Mama said. "She had to outfox the devil."

"You know, not everything has to be strictly about Kwanzaa," I explained. "The festival is really a celebration of African-American culture."

"Mm-hm," Aunt Cecelia grunted. "And you couldn't have picked something a little more serious?"

I shrugged. "Well, this is a folktale. The hero is a little girl. The kids'll like it — "

"When I was young," Aunt Cecelia plowed on, "I played Harriet Tubman in a school play. That was educational. I still remember my speech. I memorized it in front of a mirror, so I could hone my facial expressions. I did not make one mistake. When I was through, people's eyes were red."

"That's because they'd been napping," Daddy murmured.

"Pardon me?" Aunt Cecelia said.

"Uh, they couldn't stop *clapping*," Daddy shot back.

Becca came running into the kitchen, carrying a huge collage on a sheet of oaktag. Squirt followed close behind.

"Ta-da!" Becca sang, holding up her artwork.

It was a collection of toy and clothing advertisements from catalogs and magazines.

They were carefully cut up and pasted closely together, with the prices circled in red. Loops of rolled-up masking tape were on the back.

"Now no one has to ask me what I want for Christmas," she exclaimed. "It'll be right here in the kitchen."

"Who-o-o-oa," Daddy said. "Santa's going to need extra reindeer, just for you."

"No such thing," Becca announced, pressing the sheet onto the kitchen wall.

"What are you doing?" Aunt Cecelia bellowed. "Do you know how hard it is to get rid of tape marks? Your parents spent good money on that wallpaper."

"It's all right, Cecelia," Mama said gently.

"Oh?" Aunt Cecelia snapped. "Who's the one who will have to scrub off the glue when that poster is removed?"

Daddy took a deep breath. "Cecelia, I'll do it. It's the holidays, remember? The season for love and compassion?"

"And the season for spoiling small children, too, I suppose?"

"Excuse me?" Daddy asked.

Aunt Cecelia turned to leave the kitchen. "I'll wash John Philip's hands."

*"Excuse me?"*

Uh-oh. Daddy was using the Boom voice. It's so loud, it must begin down at his toes. The last time I'd heard it was the time Becca flushed a twenty-dollar bill down the toilet.

Aunt Cecelia turned back around. "I said, I'll wash — "

"No, before that!" Daddy barked.

Mama put her hand on Daddy's shoulder. "John, it's okay."

"I'll take down the poster," Becca volunteered.

"You will not!" Daddy retorted. "Jessica, Rebecca, will you please go to the family room?"

Zoom. We were out of there in a nanosecond. We shut the family room door and pressed our ears to it.

"Cecelia, this house belongs to me and my family," Daddy began. "You are living here as a guest — "

"Guest?" Aunt Cecelia huffed. "For heaven's sake, John, I am your sister!"

"Of course you are, Cecelia," Mama interrupted. "And we all love you — "

"But like it or not, you must *abide* by the rules of our house," Daddy went on, "not *make* them. We decide how our walls are treated. And more importantly, we decide how our children should be raised. You are not their mother."

"All right, John," Aunt Cecelia snapped. "You've made your point."

"Look, Cecelia, I don't mean to lose my temper," Daddy said firmly, "but I would like to see some changes around here. Loosen up with the kids. Don't expect them to be perfect, miniature grown-ups. Keep them from harm, guide them — but allow them to be kids, to make a mistake here and there."

"John," Aunt Cecelia replied softly, "you're expecting me to be somebody I'm not."

"No," said Daddy. "I am asking that you do that as long as you live in this house."

# CHAPTER 5

Thursday

Well, I met Omar Harris today. He's so full of energy. It's always fun to sit for someone totally new.

And he has so many friends. In fact, I met them. All of them. We had an eventful day.

Does anybody know how to remove glitter from your scalp?

Mary Anne is so polite. If I had been sitting that day, I'd be pulling my hair out.

And not because of the glitter.

The Harrises are an African-American family who live in Stoneybrook. Omar is seven years old, and his brother, Ebon, is six. An aunt lives with them, too, like Aunt Cecelia. She usually baby-sits, so none of us had sat for the boys before. On that day, though, the aunt was visiting relatives.

Mary Anne thought: new client. Not used to non-family sitters. Possible shyness. Clinginess. Tantrums.

She went to the job prepared. She brought along a Kid-Kit, stocked with appropriate stuff. She told herself not to take it personally if the kids had separation anxiety.

When Mr. and Mrs. Harris met her at the door, she was all smiles.

"Hello, I'm Mary Anne Sp — "

"Yeeaaaaaa, the baby-sitter!" A small boy darted toward her and grabbed her hand. "You're helping with the Kwanzaa festival."

"It's nice to meet you," Mrs. Harris said. "Now, we do have a no-TV rule on school days — "

"Come on!" Omar was trying to yank Mary Anne across the living room. "We can do some Kwanzaa stuff now!"

46

"Uh, Omar?" Mrs. Harris said. "Would you mind giving us a chance to meet the young woman?"

Omar dropped Mary Anne's hand. "I'll call my friends! They can come over, too."

"Art projects are fine," Mrs. Harris continued. "It's okay to have friends over, no sugary snacks before dinner . . . "

As the parents rambled on, Ebon quietly walked in. He stood at his mother's side, shyly staring at Mary Anne.

Mary Anne smiled to reassure him.

He walked toward her and wrapped his arms around her legs. "You're nice."

Two for two. So much for new client-itis.

The Harrises left, and Omar raced in from the kitchen. "They're coming! They're coming! Okay, what are we going to do?"

"Uh, well, I don't really know that much about Kwanzaa yet," Mary Anne said. "The first get-together for the festival is this Saturday — "

"We have books," Ebon exclaimed. "Come on."

Mary Anne followed the boys into the family room. They ran straight for the bookshelf, which lined one entire wall.

Omar grabbed two books: *The Seven Days of Kwanzaa*, by Angela Shelf Medearis, and *Crafts for Kwanzaa*, by Kathy Ross.

Mary Anne opened one of the books and began leafing through it. Ebon stopped her at a page that described how to make a *mkeke* mat, a special kind of place mat for the Kwanzaa table.

"That looks cool," he said.

Mary Anne read through the instructions. "The basic idea is to weave red and green paper strips through cuts in a sheet of black paper. So we need construction paper, glue, and scissors."

Omar and Ebon dug into an art box and pulled out all the necessary stuff. Then they went to the kitchen.

Soon, seven-year-old Sara Ford and her nine-year-old brother Marcus arrived. Then Bob and Sharelle Ingram. (He's seven and she's five.)

The Fords and the Ingrams are African-American families I didn't know well. Like the Harrises, they live in Kristy's neighborhood and attend Stoneybrook Academy, which is a private school. (Meeting new African-American Stoneybrookites was one of the nicest things about the Kwanzaa festival.)

The noise level in the kitchen had jacked up to high. Mary Anne's baby-sitting job had suddenly turned into a small day-care center.

"I do the cutting!" Marcus called.

"They're my scissors!" Omar retorted.

"So, you get to use them all the time?" Bob said.

"One at a time," Mary Anne said, picking up a sheet of black construction paper. "First of all, each of you should fold one of these in half, lengthwise."

"Ewwwww, Ebon's eating the glue!" Sharelle cried.

Ebon grinned. "It says 'nontoxic.' I was just tasting it."

"Not a good idea," Mary Anne said.

A black paper airplane whizzed by her face. Marcus was giggling like crazy.

"Marcus!" Sara yelled. "You're supposed to make mats!"

"Can I make a plane, too?" Ebon blurted out.

"Hey, cool, look at this!" Omar was pointing to a page in the book entitled "Foil Cup."

"Let's do that!" Bob cried.

"Foil cup . . . let's see . . . " Mary Anne looked at the instructions. "You need a cardboard tube from a toilet paper or paper towel roll, tinfoil, and an egg-shaped container that may be cut from an egg carton . . . "

"I can get tubes," said Ebon, running off.

Sharelle was deep into the other Kwanzaa book. "Toe puppets!" she cried out. "That's what we should make!"

Marcus dropped his latest airplane. "Let's see!"

Ta-ta-ta-taaaaaa! Mary Anne shifted into Super-Sitter mode. She glanced at the materials list on the toe puppet page. "Do you have glitter?" she asked Omar.

He nodded. "I'll get it."

"Ebon!" Mary Anne called out. "Wherever you are, we're going to need even more paper tubes."

"Okay!" Ebon replied from another room.

Mary Anne looked through the kitchen drawers and found some tinfoil for the cups. Bob grabbed it and ran to the table.

"Here's some glitter," Omar called out. Out of the corner of her eye, Mary Anne saw him throw two tubes on the table and run for the fridge.

Sharelle and Sara were taking off their shoes.

"Why are you doing that?" Mary Anne asked.

"For the toe puppets," Sara explained.

*Splat!*

Mary Anne felt some drops on her ankle. She looked down to see a raw egg splattered on the floor between her and the refrigerator.

A cry of "EWWWWWW!" went up.

The refrigerator door was ajar. Omar was

standing by it, holding an open carton of eggs. "Sorry," he said sheepishly.

"Where are the paper towels?" Mary Anne asked.

"Under the sink," Omar replied.

Mary Anne yanked open the sink cupboard, but the rack of towels was empty.

"I'll get another roll." Omar raced out of the kitchen.

Mary Anne grabbed a sponge. "Never mind."

Too late. She heard Omar's voice shouting out, "Ooooh, Ebon, you're going to get in trouble!"

Mary Anne did not like the sound of that. She dropped the sponge and ran toward the bathroom.

Omar was standing just inside the doorway. Toilet paper billowed around his ankles. Sheets of paper towel lay on the floor in huge piles.

Ebon was sitting on the closed toilet. A short and a long cardboard tube were perched on the sink. In his hands was a half-unraveled roll of paper towels.

"You wanted paper tubes," he said.

"I meant tubes that were already unrolled," Mary Anne exclaimed.

Giggles rang out from the kitchen. "Yuck!" Bob's voice called. "Marcus stepped in the egg!"

Mary Anne grabbed a handful of paper towels from the floor. As she bolted toward the kitchen, she called over her shoulder, "Please try to clean up. I'll be right back."

Back in the kitchen, a long sheet of tinfoil was now draped over the kitchen chandelier. The floor around the table was littered with cut-up, gluey construction paper. Marcus was doing a twisty dance in the egg. Bob was throwing glitter in the air like confetti.

Sara and Sharelle had taken their shoes off and were giggling.

"Phhewwwww!" Sharelle cried. "You can't put toe puppets on those stinky feet."

Poor Mary Anne.

She made Marcus take off his shoes. She wiped them off, then cleaned the floor. She asked all the kids to pick up the junk they'd dropped, and she carefully unwound the tinfoil.

Finally the kids started settling down. "Okay," Mary Anne said. "Let's see if we can try this again, calmly."

*"No, Ebon!"* Omar shouted from the bathroom. *"You're not supposed to flush paper towels down the — "*

*FOOOOOOOOOSSSSSH!*

Hoo boy.

It was one of those days.

\* \* \*

Well, guess who ended up finishing all the mats, putting the faces on the toe puppets, unclogging the toilet, and cleaning up?

Mary Anne, of course. In the middle of their projects, the kids had suddenly started whispering and giggling, then disappeared into the family room.

Mary Anne welcomed the quiet, but she became suspicious.

"Guys?" she said, leaning against the door. "What's up?"

The door opened a crack and Ebon's eyes shone through. "A project," he said.

"What kind of project?" Mary Anne asked.

"It's a surprise for Jessi," Ebon replied. "Because she's running the festival. We can't tell you what it is, or you might tell her."

Mary Anne was able to see into the room over his shoulder. It looked intact.

"No mess?" Mary Anne asked.

Omar shook his head. "Uh-uh."

Mary Anne went back to the kitchen and sank into the chair. A spray of glitter fell from her hair and onto her shirt.

I wouldn't have blamed Mary Anne if, at that moment, she wished Kwanzaa never existed.

But she got over it.

Mary Anne is a good sport.

# CHAPTER 6

"Siiiilent niiiiight . . ." sang the Washington Mall speaker system.

"Keep in line, please!" yelled an elf. "Santa's not going anywhere."

"I'm hungry!" yelled Becca.

"Doooss," demanded Squirt.

"Just a minute, please," said Aunt Cecelia.

"Excuse me!" a mom yelled. "Uh, hello, elf? How many Santas are on duty today?"

Welcome to the magical world of North Pole Village.

The music was way wrong for the occasion. It wasn't nighttime, and it sure wasn't silent. Washington Mall was jumping with holiday activity.

Actually, I adore the NPV. It appears like magic every holiday season inside Lear's department store at the far end of the mall. You step through the Wonderland Gate and onto a narrow path that twists through a snow-covered fantasy land. Little wooden huts line the path. Some of them are make-believe factories, where mechanical elves busily make toys. One hut is a reindeer stable and another is a post office stuffed with letters (a postal elf's eyes and head emerge from the pile and then sink back in).

I've always wondered what exactly is in that area of Lear's during the rest of the year. No one seems to know. Personally, I think it becomes a pocket of antimatter, invisible to the human eye. But later for that.

On Sunday morning, Aunt Cecelia, Becca, Squirt, and I were standing before the Wonderland Gate, waiting to see Santa.

Squirt was too young to know who Santa is. And Becca still insisted she didn't believe in him. So why were we there?

"Just in case," as Becca would say.

Besides, it's so cool.

Aunt Cecelia reached into the diaper bag that hung from the handles of the stroller. She pulled out a bottle full of apple juice and a small box of crackers.

"Here you go, sweethearts," she said, handing the box to Becca and the bottle to Squirt. "Would you like something, Jessica?"

"No, thanks, I'm still full from breakfast," I replied.

"Well, we have plenty of snack food," Aunt

Cecelia said, "if you change your mind."

No, you are not mistaken. That was the voice of my aunt. Hard to believe, huh?

I know how you feel. I was still numb from the shock. Aunt Cecelia had been nice to us all day. She hadn't even yelled at us in the car.

At first I thought she was just tired. Then I thought she was sick.

Finally the real reason dawned on me. Daddy's lecture. Aunt Cecelia was taking him seriously. She was turning over a new leaf.

Good-bye, grouch. So long, sourpuss.

Hello, the New Aunt Cecelia.

I guess I should have been thrilled. But to be honest, I felt worried and nervous. I needed to be home by twelve o'clock for my very first Kwanzaa festival meeting. Mallory and I planned to begin rehearsing our script of *Malindy*, which we had written the day before.

The trip to Washington Mall was supposed to have been short and sweet. But it took us forever to leave the house. Now it was 10:20, and the line was already humongous.

"Maybe we can come back another day?" I suggested.

"No way!" Becca said. "Christmas is in ten days. We have to put in our order to Santa now!"

"Ahem." I raised an eyebrow. "Our *order*?"

"Well, you know," Becca mumbled, looking away. "I mean, just for fun."

Aunt Cecelia chuckled. Squirt slurped away at his bottle. The loudspeakers were telling us to sleep in heavenly peace.

Our line inched forward every few minutes, then stopped. Talk about slow. It made a drive with Aunt Cecelia feel like the Indy 500. All the little huts kind of lost their cuteness after awhile.

I had the urge to do something really, really bad. Like climb onto one of the reindeer or open some of the letters in the post office. Just to test Aunt Cecelia.

But I didn't. I remained well behaved.

I also grew very, very bored. By the time we reached Santa, Squirt was fast asleep. I took his bottle and packed it in his diaper bag.

"Ho ho ho!" Santa said. "Excited to see me, isn't he?"

"Hi," Becca said nonchalantly, "I want a new bike with chrome wheels and tassels and one of those horns that goes *oooo*-gah, and also a board game called Guess It and a new cotton sweater like the one my sister has . . . "

I was beginning to fidget. I knew Becca's list. I'd heard it several times. Well, most of it. It seemed to grow by the hour. If she were going to recite the whole thing, we'd be holding up the line until January.

Up until then I'd been pretty confident about making the Kwanzaa festival meeting. Now I wasn't so sure.

*Click*, went the photographer's camera.

(You should see the picture. Becca's blabbering away, I'm looking down at my watch, and Squirt is slumped in the stroller, face all scrunched and mouth hanging open.)

We managed to tear Becca away eventually, but it was already after eleven.

"I'm hungry!" Becca said.

Aunt Cecelia began reaching into the diaper bag. "Would you like — "

"Not those yucky crackers," Becca whined. "I want lunch at Friendly's!"

"Becca," I said patiently, "the meeting starts soon."

"A short lunch!"

"We can't!"

*"We can!"*

*"We can't!"*

*"WAAAAHHHHHH!"* (Guess who woke up?)

"Friendly's will have to wait until the next time," Aunt Cecelia said, rummaging around in the diaper bag for Squirt's bottle. "Your sister needs to return home and your brother needs a proper nap."

"No fair!" cried Becca over Squirt's wailing.

Me? I was booking.

We bustled into the parking garage. Aunt Cecelia had not parked in a handicapped spot, so we had to walk a long way.

It was 11:15 when the car puttered onto the street. Squirt took the bottle out of his mouth. "Nomo!" (Translation: *No more left.*)

"When we go home — " Aunt Cecelia began.

"Mo! Mo!" Squirt insisted. (Translation: *I want more.*)

Uh-oh. He was early for his noon hunger crisis. Which gave us only one option until we reached home: distract him.

Becca began tickling him. "Squirty wirty-wirty-wirt!"

He kind of whined and giggled at the same time.

I turned around, adjusting the shoulder strap of my seat belt. Then I hid behind the headrest for a moment and popped out. "Boo!"

Squirt giggled a little more. But he was still squirming in his car seat, pushing against the harness.

We kept trying to make him laugh. No dice. Squirt cried louder and louder.

As for Aunt Cecelia, she was driving at turtle speed, her jaw clenched tight.

"We're almost there, Squirt," I said.

"Aaaagh . . . *aaaaaaagh!*" Squirt pushed and pushed, grunting with the effort.

"He wants to undo the harness," Becca said.

"He won't have to be in it much longer," I reassured her.

"But it's hurting him!" Becca insisted.

"Becca, we can't take it off," I said. "It's not safe."

"*EEEEEEEEEEEE!*" Squirt shrieked.

Aunt Cecelia let out a big sigh. "Jessica," she said, "you may go ahead and take the belt off. We're close to home."

Poor Squirt. I knew he was supposed to be belted at all times, but Aunt Cecelia was driving about as fast as a walk, and he looked so miserable.

I reached back and snapped loose the buckle on his belt.

Squirt pushed it aside as if he were battling off a dreaded beast.

"Feel better?" Becca asked.

Squirt took a deep breath. A smile crept across his face. "Beh . . . tah."

"He said my name!" Becca squealed.

Ahead of us, the light turned yellow. Aunt Cecelia was close to the intersection. If she were Daddy or Mama, she'd have sailed right through.

But the New Aunt Cecelia is the same kind

of driver as the old one. She stepped on the brake.

The car came to a slow stop.

*HONNNNNNNNK!!*

At first I thought the horn was Aunt Cecelia's. I couldn't see any other car on the road.

But the sound was too loud. Too deep.

And right behind us.

I heard the crash a split second before I felt it. It was a dull crack. Not like the loud *ka-boom* you hear on TV.

I shot forward. Aunt Cecelia did, too. As if we were doing some strange precision dance. It felt as if someone had sneaked up and smacked my back with an iron bat.

And then I must have blacked out, because the next thing I knew, the road had turned.

At least it seemed that way. The light was no longer in front of us. It was to my right. We were in the middle of the intersection. Stopped.

*Accident.*

The word flashed across my thoughts. The reality rushed in like a wave.

Aunt Cecelia's right hand was across my chest, as if she were trying to stop my forward movement. As if the crash hadn't yet happened. She was panting, her eyes buggy.

*Becca. Squirt.*

I spun around.

My sister was clutching her stomach in the backseat. Her face had an expression I'd never seen before. Pain, fear, shock, and confusion were all racing like shadows across her face.

Beside her, the car seat was empty.

"Squirt!" I screamed.

I couldn't see him. The window beside his seat was cracked but not enough for him to have passed through.

I tried to rise to my knees, but my seat belt held me down. Quickly I unbuckled it and turned around.

Squirt was on the floor. Lying on his side. I could only see his back and his feet. His face was in the shadow of the front seat.

He was not moving.

"SQUIIIIIIRT!" The shriek seemed to come from all around me, but I knew it was mine.

I pushed open the door. I jumped out of the car and threw the front seat forward.

Becca was crying hysterically, yelling something over and over that I couldn't understand. Aunt Cecelia was outside the car now, too, on the other side, looking in.

Now I could see all of my brother. His hands were over his face, as if he were trying to hide.

"*Is he dead is he dead is he dead?*" Becca was shrieking.

He wasn't. That was the first thing I noticed. His little chest was moving steadily.

"No," I said. "But don't touch him. If his spine is hurt, you could make him worse."

In a tiny, fragile voice, Aunt Cecelia was singing the song she uses to comfort Squirt at night: "Hush, little baby, don't say a word; Auntie's gonna buy you a mockingbird . . . "

Outside, a crowd of people was forming around us. Behind us, a man was emerging from a large red car.

"You okay?" he asked.

*"Get an ambulance!"* I yelled.

A woman in a down coat stepped forward. "I called one from my cell phone," she said. "Is someone badly hurt?"

*"My baby brother!"* I felt as if all my organs — my heart, my lungs, everything inside me — were made out of glass that was cracking.

I ducked back into the car. I ran my fingers through Squirt's hair. He felt warm, as if he were napping.

*AWWWWWWWWRRRRRRRR.*

The ambulance screeched to a stop beside us. Before I knew it a medic was in the car, yelling, "Baby!" over his shoulder. With quick but gentle motions he felt Squirt's pulse and lifted him slowly out of the car.

Another medic ran to the car with a small stretcher. As Squirt was set down onto it, his eyes seemed to focus.

He looked blankly at the medic. Then he

looked at me. Aunt Cecelia raced to my side and said, "Oh, great glory," under her breath.

"WaaaaaaAAAAAAHHHHHHHH!" Squirt's cry started low and quickly became a siren. He looked absolutely petrified.

For the first time I began to cry.

"Will he be all right?" Aunt Cecelia asked.

"I don't think anything's broken," the medic replied. "But he did black out, so we need to have him examined. How about the rest of you?"

"We all — " Aunt Cecelia's voice caught in her throat. "We all had our belts on."

"Well, I think you had better come in anyway."

By now, two police cars had pulled up. An officer walked over to Aunt Cecelia and said, "The keys are in the car, ma'am. We'll take it to the station. Now, if you'd like us to contact family . . . "

Aunt Cecelia talked to the police as I helped Becca out of the car. She was shaking uncontrollably.

I practically had to carry her into the back of the ambulance. Aunt Cecelia sat next to Squirt and held his hand.

I hugged Becca tight as the ambulance sped to the hospital. Over the muffled noise of the siren, I could hear Aunt Cecelia singing to Squirt.

Slowly his cries softened into whimpers. Then his eyes closed, and he fell into a peaceful sleep.

I took one of his hands and said, "Squirt, you're going to be all right."

I prayed it was the truth.

# CHAPTER 7

"My baby!"

Those were Mama's first words when she and Daddy burst into the examining room.

Even though the doctor was taking my blood pressure, Mama threw her arms around me.

I was a little embarrassed. But boy, was I happy to see them. Tears started running down my cheeks.

"How are you feeling, Jessi?" Daddy asked.

"Fi— " Sniff. "Fine," I replied. "Where's Squirt?"

"In another room," Mama said. "Asleep. The doctors want to give him some tests. We're supposed to stay in the waiting room."

"Well, this young lady can join you," the doctor said. "A few bruises, but everything checks out normal. It's a good thing she was wearing her seat belt."

My stomach clenched up. I began sobbing.

Mama and Daddy gently walked me out of the examining room and down the hallway. "You're okay, honey," Mama kept saying, through her own tears.

"You were lucky," Daddy said. "You could have slid into oncoming traffic."

"I wasn't lucky, I was stupid!" I blurted out. "The whole thing was my fault."

We entered the waiting room. A few people were sitting in a corner, watching a football game on TV. Daddy, Mama, and I sat together on a sofa.

"It wasn't your fault, Jessi," Daddy said softly. "The police told us what happened. The car behind you should have been keeping a safe distance — "

"*I* was the one who unbuckled Squirt," I said. "I knew I shouldn't have, but I did."

I explained it all — Squirt's crying, Becca's pleading, Aunt Cecelia's giving me permission. Daddy and Mama sat listening, their faces growing grim.

By the time I finished, Becca was walking into the room, escorted by an unfamiliar doctor. "Your daughter's a little shaken," he said, "but physically fine."

Becca buried herself in Mama's arms, weeping.

Moments later, Aunt Cecelia walked in. She was limping a little, and she had a bandage on her chin. Her mouth was trembling and she looked at Daddy with watery eyes. I'd never seen her look so old and meek.

Daddy stood up and guided Aunt Cecelia toward the sofa.

"Ohh," she said, "I'm so glad you're here. How are the girls?"

"We're fine, Aunt Cecelia," I replied.

"Thank goodness," she said, sitting down. "Have they said anything about John Philip?"

"Not yet," Daddy replied. "How are you?"

"I cut my chin on the steering wheel and twisted my back a bit, but no other damage." Aunt Cecelia sighed deeply. "Of course, I'm the one who deserves to be in that examining room right now. I told Jessi to unbuckle him. I don't know what got into me."

For the first time in my life, I saw Aunt Cecelia start to cry. Mama and Daddy both put their arms around her.

We sat silently for awhile. A clock on the wall said 11:49. Only a half hour had passed since the accident. It had felt like ages.

*Eleven forty-nine?*

The Kwanzaa festival meeting! I had totally forgotten about it. It was supposed to begin in eleven minutes.

No way could I go to it. Not with my baby brother in the examining room. I needed to call Mallory.

I explained the situation to Mama and Daddy. Then I ran to a nearby pay phone and tapped out the Pikes' number.

Mallory was shocked. I could hear her crying as I described what had happened. Then she asked me a million questions. I kept having to put extra coins in the phone. Eventually an official-sounding voice behind me called out, "Mr. and Mrs. Ramsey?"

A doctor was standing by the waiting room entrance, holding a clipboard. She was smiling warmly.

"Yes?" Mama said.

"I'm Dr. Bradley," she said. "Would you all follow me, please? Your little boy is very eager to see you."

I told Mallory I had to go, then hung up.

Dr. Bradley led us down a brightly lit corridor. When we turned the first corner, Squirt's scream echoed from a distant room.

My heart jumped. We all quickened our steps.

When Dr. Bradley reached the doorway to an examination room, she announced, "Here they are!"

Squirt was lying on a crib bed, strapped down. One of his little arms was connected to an IV tube.

"Hi, Squirt," we all called out.

"Mama . . ." Squirt looked around in

amazement, as if he'd given up ever seeing us again. "Daddoo . . . See-lah . . . Bet-tah!"

"Heyyyy, what about me?" I said.

Squirt looked at me and grinned wide. "Dooooss!"

Mama, Daddy, and Becca laughed. (I wasn't sure why I reminded him of juice, but I didn't care.) Squirt giggled and clapped his hands. I could tell he was trying to rise from the bed, but he couldn't.

The poor little guy. He must have thought his whole life was about *straps*. Strapped into the car seat, strapped into the bed . . .

I had to choke back a sob. If I hadn't undone the strap in the car, he wouldn't have to be struggling with this one.

"John Philip will be just fine," Dr. Bradley reassured us, "but he did hit his head, and I'm picking up some unusual neurological activity on the EEG. I'm concerned he may have had a concussion, so I'd like to admit him and keep him here for observation for a few days — "

"A few days!" Mama exclaimed.

"What do you mean, 'unusual activity'?" Daddy asked.

"It may be nothing," Dr. Bradley replied. "A child's system is immature, and the charts are sometimes erratic even with normal readings. But if I have even the slightest doubt, I like to take all precautions."

"But who's he going to play with?" Becca asked.

"We do happen to have three other children in the hospital," Dr. Bradley explained. "I'll arrange for them to be close together. For awhile, John will have to be bedridden, but the company of other children may comfort him."

Daddy nodded grimly. Aunt Cecelia started wringing her hands.

Mama was gently stroking Squirt's hair, but she looked fiercely at Dr. Bradley. "He's so little, Doctor. He'll need one of us. I noticed your visiting hours are — "

"Don't pay attention to those," Dr. Bradley said. "For young children we bend the rules. You can pretty much stay as long as you like during the day."

"Eeeeee!" Squirt was pushing against his strap now.

"Can you undo that?" Mama asked.

Memories of the crash came back, and I wanted to shout, "No!" But Dr. Bradley calmly unstrapped Squirt and let him sit up. "He shouldn't leave the bed yet," she said, "but when I unhook the IV later when he's in his room, you can hold him in your lap."

Dr. Bradley stayed with us a few more minutes, then went off to see another patient. We were alone with Squirt now. He was drinking his bottle and looked pretty happy.

"I want one of us to be here with him at all times," Mama said firmly.

Daddy nodded. "Let's work out a schedule of shifts."

"Squirt shifts," Becca said.

"Daddy and I will try to take some personal days off from work," Mama went on. "Cecelia can visit while you girls are in school, and you can join us afterward if you like."

"Can we take personal days from school?" Becca asked.

Daddy smiled. "Nice try."

We stayed for a few hours after Squirt was checked in, planning our visits, playing with Squirt, trying hard to be cheerful.

Around dinnertime, Mama agreed to stay with Squirt while the rest of us went home. (Actually, she ordered us.)

Daddy, Becca, Aunt Cecelia, and I walked out of the hospital together. We hardly said a word to each other. I felt drained and tired.

We piled into the car, Becca and I in the back, Daddy and Aunt Cecelia in front.

As Daddy pulled onto the road, Aunt Cecelia looked very nervous. "Use your signals, John," she said.

No, Daddy did not yell. Instead he said, "Oh, sorry," and flicked the signal lever.

"Please don't drive fast," she went on.

"I won't," Daddy replied.

"And be careful at yellow lights."

"Uh-huh."

Aunt Cecelia began shaking her head. "I'm sorry, John. I'm nagging you."

"It's all right," Daddy said with a sigh. "Maybe I should listen to you more often."

Becca and I gave each other a Look. It was as if Daddy had said the sky was green.

"I'm just an old sourpuss," Aunt Cecelia said. "I can't even look after my own nephew."

"Oh, yes you can, Cecelia," Daddy replied. "I know you. You never would have let him ride without a seat belt. You were trying to be lenient. You were trying to ease up with the kids. Who told you to do that? Me. If I hadn't opened my big mouth, Squirt would be home now."

"Uh-uh, Daddy," Becca said quietly. "I was bothering Aunt Cecelia. I told her Squirt should be unbuckled."

"Neither of you unstrapped him," I grumbled. "I did."

"Hush," Daddy said. "All of you. It happened. We can't change that now. Let's just be grateful he's alive and recovering."

Daddy pulled to a stop at a red light on Kimball Street. Snow was beginning to fall. A few neighborhood kids were running around on a white-dusted lawn, trying to catch snowflakes on their tongues, while their mom

73

and dad strung Christmas lights on the porch. The parents waved to us.

I think we waved back. I don't remember for sure.

Our minds were a million miles away from the holidays.

# CHAPTER 8

CAPTAIN'S LOG,
   STARDATE 12/15

Okay, I should
say "acting captain."
Jessi's our real
captain, but I'm
solo at the moment.
Well, maybe acting
isn't the right word.
We can't really do
much of that yet,
either.
   The kids are begin-
ning to arrive here
at the Stoneybrook
Community Center.
I won't be able to
write in this official
Kwanzaa Festival
Journal much longer.
   Whose idea was
this, anyway?
   Jessi and Mallory,
where are you? HELP!

The journal was *my* idea. I thought it would be interesting. I hadn't expected that Abby would be the one to start it.

I hadn't expected to miss the meeting, either.

Actually, Mallory and I were going to run the first meeting ourselves. But Abby had insisted on helping out. She didn't have a sitting job that day, and she was really excited about the Kwanzaa festival.

It was a good thing, too, because she was the only BSC member there at noon.

"There" was a medium-size room at the Stoneybrook Community Center, just down the hall from the big conference room we'd reserved for the festival.

Abby had come to the center earlier to play basketball. As she waited, she practiced her dribbling.

"Oh, cool!" a voice shouted.

Abby turned to see two young boys running toward her. Their dad was behind them.

"Omar!" he called out. "Ebon! This isn't the right place. Come on!"

"Mr. Harris?" Abby said.

"Yes." Mr. Harris looked a little startled. "Have we met?"

Abby extended her hand. "Nope. But I've heard all about your boys. I'm Abby Stevenson. I'm helping out with the Kwanzaa festival."

"Ohhhh!" Mr. Harris cleared his throat. "I'm sorry. When I said it was the wrong room, I meant, you know, I was expecting Jessi Ramsey, and — "

"No sweat," Abby said. "If I saw you in a synagogue, I might be a little confused, too."

They both burst out laughing. Omar and Ebon were now passing a ball around and bouncing it off a wall.

Before long Sara and Marcus showed up with their mom. Then Bob and Sharelle Ingram. And Tomika Batts and Ronnie Olatunji and Duane Hicks.

As the parents said good-bye and wandered off, a basketball game started.

"Score!" Omar threw the ball against the wall into an imaginary net.

The ball bounced off the wall and hit Sharelle in the head. "Owwwww!"

Bob grabbed the ball. "You missed! That bounced off the backboard."

"Did not!" Omar said.

"Did too!" Bob replied.

"Guys — " Abby began.

The door opened and Mallory flew in, all out of breath. "Sorry I'm late!"

"Well, it's about time," Abby snapped.

"Jessi called me from the hospital," Mal said, throwing her coat on a table. "She's been in an accident."

Abby turned pale. "Whaaaat?"

In a breathless rush, Mallory told her what had happened. All the kids gathered around, listening silently. Sharelle started to cry.

"Where is she?" Abby demanded. "Can I talk to her?"

"She's still at the hospital," Mallory replied. "She doesn't know when she's going to be leaving. She hasn't seen Squirt yet. She says *she's* fine, but she wants us to have this meeting without her."

"How can we?" Marcus asked. "She's, like, the boss."

"Did Squirt's head smash through the windshield?" Duane asked.

"Can you take us to visit them?" Ebon piped up.

The kids did not want to begin the meeting. Mallory and Abby had to comfort, explain, reassure.

Mal knew that the only way to divert their attention was to start the rehearsal. When the kids had calmed down a little, she pulled a stack of papers from her backpack. "Jessi will be upset if we don't start working on the play. I made copies for all those who can read."

Suddenly nine pairs of hands shot toward her.

"One at a time!" Abby shouted.

"You can't read!" Marcus said to Ebon.

"Can too!" Ebon snapped. "I read *Hop on Pop*!"

"I call I'm Malindy!" Bob shouted.

Omar howled with laughter. "Malindy's a girl!"

"How do you know?" Bob asked. "It's a fake name, so it can go either way."

"Is it a comedy show?" Ronnie asked.

"I want to sing 'The Colors of the Wind,' " Tomika insisted.

"The most talented one plays Malindy," Marcus called out. "That's me!"

"Can I do a tap dance?" Duane asked.

"I-I-I-I'm the de-e-evil!" Omar croaked in a scratchy voice.

"Can you paaaaiint with all the co-o-o-lors . . . " Tomika warbled.

Abby let out a loud whistle. "Guys, please! This is a Kwanzaa play. Not a variety show."

"We have enough parts for everyone," Mallory said. "Now, Malindy happens to be a girl. And I'd like Sharelle to play her — "

"Ohhhhhh . . . " Sara and Tomika groaned.

"— as a young girl," Mallory quickly added. "But she grows older in the play. Sara will play

Malindy as a big girl, and Tomika will play her as a young woman."

The girls puffed up with pride.

"We'll also need a brother and a father for Malindy," Mallory went on, "a sheep who cracks jokes, a pig who eats and rolls around in the mud, a barking dog . . . "

I should explain. None of those parts are actually in the story. Mallory and I invented them, to give all the kids something fun to play.

"I'm the pig!" Bob cried out.

Sharelle started cracking up. "We already know that!"

"I want to be the dog," Duane said. "He doesn't have to sing or anything, right?"

"Beeeeaaaaaah," bleated Ebon. "Why did the bubble gum cross the road? Beeeeeahhh!"

"Arrrrgh!" Omar growled in his devil voice. "I'm going to cook you for dinner."

"Give up?" Ebon asked. "It's because — "

"Hey, I'm the devil!" Marcus claimed.

"Hmmm," Mallory said, "I need *someone* to play Malindy's strong, bossy older brother who kicks the devil away."

"Me!" Marcus shot back.

"Because — " Ebon tried again.

"What about me?" Ronnie asked.

"The mischievous younger brother?" Mallory suggested.

Ronnie nodded. "Okay."

"*Because,*" Ebon shouted above the din, "*it was stuck to the chicken's foot!*"

Sara gave him a Look. "What are you talking about?"

"Get it?" Ebon pressed on. "The chicken crossed the road, and — "

"Okay, let's sit in a circle and read the lines," Abby said. "No staging yet."

Giggling with excitement, the kids plopped themselves right down.

"All right," Mallory said, "at the beginning of the play, Malindy is skipping across the stage with Rex, her dog."

"Rex?" Duane asked. "That's a dinosaur name."

"Ooh! I know!" Marcus spoke up. "See, Malindy is living in Jurassic Park . . . "

"Rrrrrawwwwrrr!" Duane bellowed.

"Use the script!" Abby shouted.

I don't know how Abby and Mallory managed it. It took them about ten minutes just to start reading.

Things didn't improve afterward. Tomika insisted she should have a song. Marcus kept shouting his lines at the top of his lungs. Ebon, who couldn't read well yet, made up his own lines. Bob the pig and Duane the dog switched roles. And Ronnie kept insisting he wanted to be a penguin.

By the time the parents began arriving, the kids had finally settled down and were reading well. They received a wild ovation.

Mallory and Abby were exhausted as the families trickled out. "Can we call Jessi at the hospital?" Abby asked.

Mallory shook her head. "We shouldn't bother her there. She said she'd call me this afternoon."

"I think she'd be proud of how the meeting went." Abby looked at her Kwanzaa sheet. "We experienced all these Kwanzaa things ourselves. Unity, creativity, collective work and responsibility, purpose . . . five of them in one shot."

"Six," Mallory said softly.

"What's the other?"

Mallory's eyes began to water. She was thinking about Squirt, hoping he would pull through all right.

When she spoke, her voice was barely above a whisper. "Faith."

# CHAPTER 9

"Hungry?" Daddy asked.

"Nahh," I replied.

"Me neither."

That was practically our whole conversation on the way home from the hospital that Friday. The accident had happened only five days before, but the trip felt like our thousandth.

Pale yellow light from the street lamps washed over Daddy's face in a slow rhythm. His eyes were narrow slits. Boy, did he look tired.

I didn't blame him. He and Mama hadn't slept much over the previous few days. Fortunately, they'd both managed to take off the whole week from their offices. Unfortunately, they still had to turn in their work, using the fax machine and Fed Ex. Because they were spending so much time at the hospital, often they worked late into the night.

I did, too. It was the only way I could finish my homework. That week I'd spent every spare after-school minute at the hospital — when I wasn't at BSC meetings, a sitting job, and two Kwanzaa festival rehearsals.

I hadn't slept well, either. We were all worried about Squirt. He had blacked out a couple of times, and Dr. Bradley wanted him to stay longer.

For two whole days Squirt had to be hooked up to electrodes. Yes, I am serious. Long wires were glued to his scalp and attached to a pack around his waist. The doctor said it was the only way to do accurate readings. My little brother looked like something out of a horror movie. I was a basket case when I first saw him.

It didn't help that he kept saying, "Home? Home?" whenever one of us stood up to leave.

On that day, Friday, I had skipped the BSC meeting (with Kristy's permission). Daddy had picked me up straight from school and taken me to the hospital. After awhile we'd started talking about holiday shopping. We'd hardly done any, and now Christmas was only five days away. Mama declared we'd do it all that night.

Which is why Daddy and I were driving home. We were going to pick up Aunt Cecelia and Becca, then return to the hospital around

Squirt's bedtime to pick up Mama. Then we would go shopping.

(Complicated, huh? Our whole week had been like this.)

Daddy pulled to a stop in front of the house. As we trudged inside, Becca greeted us in the front hallway.

"Doe bore pedcils, doe bore books," she sang. "Doe bore teachers' dirty looks!"

"Rebecca, you get away from that open door!" Aunt Cecelia called from the kitchen. "You are coming down with something."

"I lo-o-o-ove vacatiod!" Becca screamed, skipping back inside.

Vacation.

Today had been the last day of school before the holidays. I'd almost forgotten.

I always adore the first day of a vacation. It feels so free and exhilarating.

Not this year. Part of me was worrying about Squirt. Part was thinking about Christmas gifts. Part was worrying how on earth I was going to pull together the festival.

Aunt Cecelia bustled in, looking at her watch. "Your sister-in-law is on the phone, John. Where were you? I expected you home half an hour ago."

"Sorry, sergeant," Daddy grumbled. "Next time I'll just race out when my son is clinging to me and begging to go home. 'I have to meet Cecelia's schedule,' I'll say."

As he stomped away toward the kitchen phone, Aunt Cecelia said, "No need to be sarcastic."

"He's tired," I explained to Aunt Cecelia.

"Well, that's no excuse," Aunt Cecelia replied. "We *all* are!"

"Hi, Yvonne," Daddy was saying into the phone. "Hanging in. . . . He'll be back to normal soon. . . . I don't know how many. . . . Mm-hm, listen, we have to leave again and I have to go find a shopping list. . . . Not now, all right? Listen, I'm sure Jessi would love to speak to Keisha . . . "

I ran inside. I'd spoken to Keisha only once since the accident, and I was dying to hear her voice.

Daddy handed me the receiver and headed upstairs toward his room. "Hi!" I said.

"Hi," Keisha answered softly. "Mom told me about Squirt. Too bad he's not home yet, huh?"

"Yeah, but he'll be here when you guys come to town."

Keisha was silent for a moment. "Yeah . . . well, the thing is . . . I mean, maybe we can see you all in February. Mom says we're going to stay home for Kwanzaa."

I felt as if I'd been slapped in the face. "Stay home? But why? You said you were coming."

"I know. But Mom and Dad say you have too much to think about, with Squirt in the hospital."

*Click.*

Daddy had picked up the phone extension in his room. "Hello, Keisha?" he said. "Excuse me, sweetheart, I hate to cut your conversation short, but we have to leave in a minute. Could you put your mom or dad on the phone, please?"

I didn't like the sound of that. Daddy was trying to be polite, but I could tell he was mad about something.

"Sure," Keisha said. " 'Bye, Uncle John. 'Bye, Jessi."

" 'Bye." I hung up and went to the bottom of the stairs to listen.

"Yes, hello, Yvonne, it's John again," Daddy's voice said. "What's this I hear about you not coming for Kwanzaa? . . . Uh-huh . . . No, we're fine. . . . Not at all, Yvonne. . . . Of course you're coming! I won't hear another word! . . . All right, good-bye."

Whew. Sometimes I like Daddy's bossiness. It can come in handy.

*Thump-thump-thump-thump-thump-thump.* Daddy came downstairs, calling out, "Let's go to the hospital! Put your coats on!"

"Go?" Aunt Cecelia walked into the kitchen, hands on hips. "What about dinner?"

"We'll eat out," Daddy replied.

"But I just defrosted a chicken!"

"It'll have to wait, Cecelia. Or you can stay home and eat it yourself. But the rest of us need to do some shopping."

Aunt Cecelia sucked her teeth with exasperation. "You barge in here late. You change all our evening plans without even calling to tell me. I have a sick child here on my hands — "

"I'b dot sick!" Becca insisted. "It's just a sdiffle."

"Fine." Aunt Cecelia clomped over to the counter. She grabbed a platter on which a frozen chicken sat in its plastic wrapping. "Just fine. Who needs to tell old, sick Aunt Cecelia about anything in advance? Who cares how she feels?"

As Daddy and I headed for the front door, we could hear the tinny thump of the platter as Aunt Cecelia shoved it into the fridge. Becca followed close behind us, zipping up her down jacket.

We waited about five minutes in the car. Finally Aunt Cecelia emerged from the house, a sullen expression on her face. She walked slowly down the front path toward us.

"Cecelia, come along!" Daddy called out the window. "We don't have all night."

Aunt Cecelia didn't change her pace one bit. The moment she sat in the passenger seat and closed the door, Daddy drove off like a shot.

"John, you haven't changed since you were a child," Aunt Cecelia said. "You never could plan a thing — "

"*Plan?*" Daddy thundered. "My son is in the hospital, I'm trying to provide for this family, working at night, with the holidays around the corner — and you're talking about a *plan?* It's all I can do just to shepherd this family from day to day. If you had used your brains in the car last week, none of this would have happened in the first place."

"I was acting under your threat! If you hadn't insisted I spoil the children — "

"*AUUUGGGH!*" Daddy pounded the steering wheel.

I nearly jumped out of my seat. I thought Daddy was going to slug his own sister.

"*I forgot my list of gifts!*" Daddy exclaimed.

"Well, then, let's go back," Aunt Cecelia said.

Daddy shook his head. "No, we're late as it is. We won't have enough time to shop. I'll just piece the list together from memory."

"Do as you like. You always do. But don't complain to me if you forget something."

The car fell silent. Aunt Cecelia and Daddy were like two stone statues.

Becca and I just sank further and further into our seats.

# CHAPTER 10

"Rraaaaaaagggh!" roared Ebon Harris.

"Yikes!" Mary Anne jumped back from her front door, holding her heart dramatically.

Ebon ripped off his African mask. "It's just me!"

"Whew," Mary Anne replied.

Mary Anne's dad emerged from the kitchen to greet the Harrises. "Welcome. I'm Richard Spier."

The parents shook hands. Omar held up a big plastic bag. "We brought black-eyed peas for the Hoppin' John!"

"Hopping who?" Richard asked.

Omar and Ebon cackled with laughter. "It's a kind of food."

"Aha. Of course." Richard slunk into the kitchen, red-faced.

Abby, Kristy, Stacey, and I were already in

there, supervising. Tomika and Ronnie were mashing bananas (which go into Liberian rice bread). Bob and Duane were taking turns crushing peanuts with a mortar and pestle (for Ashanti peanut soup), then comparing biceps.

Have you ever eaten Hoppin' John? If you haven't, you should. It's basically black-eyed peas and rice. Simple, but you can't stop eating it.

Mary Anne was in charge of making the Hoppin' John, but she was busy greeting the Harrises. So I put a huge pot on the stove for her.

Everyone seemed so psyched. Me? I had almost called the festival off.

Squirt was still in the hospital, Aunt Cecelia was squabbling with my parents all the time, and now Becca was sick in bed.

Guess what? Her cold wasn't a cold. It was the flu.

Becca had cried when I left home to go to Mary Anne's.

I sighed and looked at the menu I'd written out: five scrumptious African-American dishes we could make and freeze for the festival. Along with the Hoppin' John and the Ashanti peanut soup, we were going to have okra with corn, Liberian rice bread, and Senegalese cookies.

Yum. My mood was beginning to lift.

With a pencil, I assigned one baby-sitter and three or four kids to each dish.

"Is everybody here?" Kristy asked.

Abby groaned. "You're not going to call us to order, are you?"

"Shout 'Here' when I call your name!" Kristy said, then read from a list: "Omar?"

"Here!"

"Ebon?"

"Me!"

"Jake Kuhn!"

"Present!"

"Patsy Kuhn!"

"President!"

Yes, the Kwanzaa festival had grown. Now we were seventeen kids strong. Our six new-comers were kids who'd heard about the group at school — the Kuhn kids, three of Mallory's siblings (nine-year-old Nicky, eight-year-old Vanessa, and seven-year-old Margo), and Rosie Wilder (seven), who agreed to play the fiddle for *Malindy and Little Devil.*

When Kristy finished taking attendance, she yelled: *"And now I give you the brains behind the Kwanzaa festival, Miiiis Jessiiiii Ramsey!"*

Everyone started hooting and clapping, even the parents who were still hanging out. I was so embarrassed.

"Um, hi," I said. (I know, *duh*, what a beginning.) "The most important rule today is, we have to save some food for Becca. She's home with the flu."

"Be-*cca!* Be-*cca!*" Marcus began chanting.

"The next thing," I went on, "is to remember we still have nine days to the festival, so don't feel that we have to do everything today."

"In other words," Abby cut in, "if you drop boogers in the soup, we can always chuck it and make some more next week."

"Ewwwww!" the kids yelled.

Some of the grown-ups looked a little queasy.

"Okay, each baby-sitter will take a group," I went on. "Five sitters, five different dishes to prepare . . . "

I read the list of foods, assigned sitters, and kids.

It went in seventeen ears and out seventeen others.

About ten kids shouted, "I want to work on cookies!"

"Why did I get peanut soup?" Sara pouted. "No fair."

"I'm switching to Hoppin' John!" Marcus announced.

"What's okra?" Jake asked.

"A vegetable," Duane and Ronnie answered.

"That grows only in Okrahoma!" Tomika shouted, cracking up.

Sharelle raised her hand. "Can we make peanut-butter-and-jelly sandwiches?"

*PHWEEEEEET!*

Leave it to Kristy. She had brought along her referee's whistle.

Total silence.

"Guys," Kristy said, "the groups are for *making* food. As far as *tasting* the food, we can all share."

"Yeeeeaaaa!"

"As long as we leave enough for the festival!" Stacey added.

I don't think anyone heard her. The kids were all racing for the kitchen.

I was in charge of the okra with corn. The recipe: chop up some okra, onions, and tomatoes, put them in a saucepan with frozen corn and some water, and cook it all up. Easy.

Or so I thought.

I hadn't imagined all the interesting uses for okra my group would discover. Marcus demonstrated that a piece of okra is just the right size to fit in a nostril. Sharelle cut off the ends of five pieces and capped her fingers with them.

I helped Vanessa chop up onions. When we started crying from the fumes, everyone thought it was hilarious. They crowded into the kitchen to stare.

"Go away!" Vanessa cried, sniffling.

"Crybaby!" Nicky shouted.

That was when a hunk of mashed banana flew into my hair.

"Oops," said Ronnie. He was standing at the counter, looking sheepish. "I was only trying to shake it off my fingers."

The kids were screaming with laughter. Nicky smeared his chin with rice cereal, which he was preparing for the bread, and started shouting, "Ho ho ho!"

Out of the corner of my eye, I could see some parents peeking from the living room. Kristy was reaching for her whistle.

Before she could blow it, I shouted, *"Hey! I can cancel this festival, you know!"*

The kids went back to work. Kristy gave me a thumbs-up sign. I smiled and wiped the onion tears from my eyes.

Somehow we managed to make all the dishes. The cookies, which are basically sugar cookies with peanut butter and chopped peanuts, all disappeared. But we had enough of the other stuff to freeze.

The kids were proud of themselves. As they were preparing to leave, I could hear them laughing and bragging to their parents.

I stayed in the kitchen, cleaning up. The

happiness was not rubbing off on me. I was still thinking about Squirt and Becca. And what they were missing.

It seemed so unfair. Squirt was in some boring hospital, not old enough to understand why. Becca, who wanted so much to enjoy the holiday, was sick in bed.

We hadn't even had a chance to buy a tree or decorate the house. By the time our family returned to normal, the season would be over.

The accident replayed in my mind. Then I imagined myself refusing to undo the buckle. Following my conscience. I imagined how the holiday would have been, happy and carefree, everybody safe and sound.

"Jessi?"

I turned at the sound of Omar's voice.

Standing in the kitchen doorway was the entire Kwanzaa gang. Some of the kids were dressed to go outside. All of them were smiling broadly.

Omar stepped forward. He held out a box wrapped in hand-decorated wrapping paper. "This is for your brother," he said. "We made it ourselves."

"It was supposed to be a surprise for you," Ebon added.

Sara rolled her eyes. *"Ebon . . ."*

"Don't open it," Tomika warned me. "Give it to Squirt in the hospital."

"With a kiss from us," Sharelle added.

I remembered Mary Anne talking about their secret gift. So this was it. I was glad they'd decided to give it to Squirt.

Tears began rolling down my cheeks. "Thanks," I squeaked.

Mary Anne stepped into the kitchen and put her arms around me.

"You ought to do something about those onions," Marcus said.

Daddy was grinning when he drove me home from the meeting. And he started whistling Christmas carols.

I had no idea why he was in such a good mood. But I didn't ask any questions. I didn't want to risk spoiling it.

When we arrived home, I saw lights twinkling through the living room window.

"You bought a tree!" I exclaimed.

He smiled. "*I* didn't."

I left the car and ran inside. The pine aroma hit me the moment I opened the door.

The tree was gorgeous — thick and perfectly shaped, reaching all the way to the ceiling. Mama and Aunt Cecelia sang hellos to me as they hung decorations.

"Jessi! Jessi!" Becca came running in from the kitchen, still in her pajamas. "Mallory brought a tree for us!"

Mallory and her dad followed Becca into the room, with trays of hot chocolate and cookies.

"You did this?" I asked.

Mallory smiled bashfully. "Do you like it?"

"I love it!" I exclaimed.

"Well, I knew you guys didn't have time to buy one. So I told Dad, and we just stopped off at the nursery."

"That's so . . . so . . . " I could barely speak for the lump in my throat. "Sweet!"

"It's the holiday spirit," Mallory said. "Christmas giving, Kwanzaa togetherness."

I couldn't think of a thing to say. My feelings were beyond words.

Mallory put her arms around me, and the tiny lights of the Christmas tree became a blur of colors.

# CHAPTER 11

"Jessica!" Daddy called from the checkout line.

There. I found what I wanted and ran.

Daddy was already loading some bananas and a box of cereal onto the conveyor belt.

I added three jars of baby food — creamed turkey, creamed sweet potatoes, and creamed green beans.

"Turkey dinner mush, huh?" Daddy said. "Too bad they didn't have creamed stuffing."

We paid quickly and ran out to the parking lot.

The supermarket was one of the only stores open on Christmas Day in the Essex Street minimall. Another was Baby and Company, two stores down. Aunt Cecelia was trundling through the exit, clutching a paper bag.

We climbed into the car, and Mama turned the key in the ignition.

"Mercy, I forgot to have them wrap the baby

slippers!" Aunt Cecelia reached for the door handle. "I'll be right back."

"No!" Mama and Daddy shouted at the same time.

Mama stepped on the gas and away we went.

We were late for the hospital, where we were going to celebrate Christmas, Part Two.

During Christmas, Part One, we'd had breakfast at home and opened presents with Becca, who was still sick. Then Daddy drove to the hospital with presents for Squirt and played Santa for the kids there.

At eleven o'clock, Mallory had come over to baby-sit for Becca. (Yes, baby-sit. On Christmas Day. Can you believe it? We hadn't even asked her. She'd just volunteered on the day that she brought over the tree.) That allowed the rest of us to visit Squirt together.

How did Becca feel about being left out? Not great. But Dr. Bradley had advised against our taking her to the hospital.

The moment Daddy arrived home we took off. I carried the present that the Kwanzaa group had made for Squirt.

We pulled into the hospital parking lot and went inside. The receptionist, who was wearing a red elf cap, waved us right in.

The hospital felt much cheerier than usual.

The Christmas tree in the waiting room had presents under it. Lots of families were visiting patients, spilling into the hallways. Cries of "Merry Christmas!" rang out everywhere.

When we reached Squirt's hallway, I sprinted to the door.

"Surpri— "

My voice caught in my throat.

Squirt was gone.

Mama, Daddy, and Aunt Cecelia walked up beside me. Their smiles vanished.

Not even his crib bed was there.

"Where is he?" Mama asked.

"Now — now — " Aunt Cecelia was starting to hyperventilate. "Don't panic!"

"Was he okay this morning?" Mama asked Daddy.

"Seemed so," Daddy replied. Then he cupped his hands over his mouth and yelled, "Nurse!"

Around the corner walked a nurse we'd come to know, named Gina. "There you are!" she called out. "Didn't they tell you?"

Mama swallowed deeply. "Tell us what?"

"Follow me," Gina replied.

She began walking briskly back down the hallway. Following her, I felt queasy. Where was she taking us? An operating room? Had something awful happened?

Gina stopped at a closed door marked Nurses' Lounge. "He'll be so happy to see you."

She pushed open the door. Inside, the furniture had been pushed aside to make room for a Christmas tree. A group of adults was gathered at a table with food and beverages. A couple of kids, about five years old, were chasing each other around the room. A small group of younger children were setting up a wooden train track near the wall. Over a set of speakers, a chorus was singing "Haaaaallelujah!"

In the corner, some nurses were playing with three babies in crib beds.

Squirt was in one of them, biting on a big rubber spider.

Boy, was I relieved. I felt as if a cement mixer had been lifted from my shoulders.

"The staff is having a little party for the children," Gina explained.

I set down the present and ran to Squirt, my arms outstretched. "Squirt! Merry Christmas!"

He looked up at me, then back down. When I reached for him, he squirmed away.

"How's my big boy?" Daddy scooped him out of the crib.

"No! No!" Squirt yelled. "Keeb! Keeb!" (That's Squirt talk for "crib.")

Daddy kissed him, then passed him to Mama and Aunt Cecelia. "Look what we brought!" Mama said. "Your favorite! Bananas!"

"And beautiful slippers," Aunt Cecelia said. "Even though your parents wouldn't let me wrap them."

"Keeb! Keeb!" Squirt repeated.

"All right, all right . . . " Mama set him down in the crib.

"Why so fussy, John Philip?" Gina said. "It's your *family!*"

I leaned into his crib and gave him his present. "This is from my friends."

Aha! A spark of interest! He grabbed it and began ripping off the beautiful hand-printed paper.

Inside was a lovely scrapbook held together with pipe cleaners. Its pages were red, black, and green construction paper, covered carefully with zippered plastic bags. Its cover was made from a brown paper bag, and it looked like this:

"Wow," said Daddy.

"Very special," agreed Mama.

"So much work," added Aunt Cecelia.

I set the book down near Squirt. He took a look.

Then he pushed it away and went back to his spider.

"Well," Gina said, "why don't we wheel him back to his room so he can have a nice, quiet visit with his family?"

She took hold of one side of the crib and began to push.

"*N-O-O-O-O-O-O!*" Squirt was reaching back toward the other kids, as if he were being taken away to prison.

"It's okay," Daddy said. "We'll stay here with him."

Gina wheeled him back. We all found metal folding chairs and sat around the crib.

"He's punishing us," Aunt Cecelia whispered.

Mama gave her a cross look. "What do you mean by that?"

"For leaving him every day," Aunt Cecelia replied.

"We have sacrificed for a week and a half to spend as much time as we can here," Daddy spoke up.

Aunt Cecelia shook her head. "Makes no difference to him."

"Cecelia, I don't see what good you are doing by casting blame!" Mama said.

Their voices were no longer whispers. I was sure the other grown-ups in the room could hear. I buried my face in my hands.

"Mr. and Mrs. Ramsey?"

I looked up. Dr. Bradley was walking into the room, smiling, as usual.

"I have news for you," she continued. "Your son's tests have stabilized. The EEG and CAT scan are consistently normal, and he's been alert and happy lately, no blackouts . . . "

I had heard speeches like this before. I knew what the next words would be. *So we'll keep him for just a few more days . . .*

"So," Dr. Bradley went on, "you will be able to take Squirt home tomorrow!"

I jumped out of my seat.

"Haaaaaaal-le-lu-jah!" blared the speakers.

Or maybe it wasn't the speakers.

Maybe it was me.

# CHAPTER 12

Thursday

HAPPY KWANZAA!
It's the day after Christmas and the first
day of Kwanzaa. Not only that, it's
Squirt's homecoming! A triple celebration
for the Ramseys!
If only the Ramseys could see it that
way. I'm sure they will, eventually.
Let me start from the beginning. I
sat for Becca this morning, while
Jessi and the grown-ups went to
pick up Squirt.
How did Becca feel about this?
Pretty rotten...

"Why do I have to stay home again?" Becca whined.

"Because Dr. Bradley said so," Daddy replied. "You still have the flu, honey."

"Dr. Bradley doesn't know everything!" With a fork Becca stabbed a clump of scrambled eggs on her breakfast plate.

Mama leaned down and gave her a hug. "Sorry, sweetheart. We'll bring Squirt home as soon as we can. Meanwhile, don't make trouble for Mallory."

"Rrrwwf," Becca grunted.

"Thanks, Mallory," I said as we headed for the door.

"You're welcome," Mallory replied. " 'Bye!"

Mallory is amazing. She knew how important this day was for us, so she insisted on baby-sitting again. She said, "Squirt might as well have as many of his family with him as he can."

"Did you have a nice Christmas dinner?" Mallory asked.

"Mmm," Becca replied.

"The Christmas tree looks beautiful," Mallory said.

"Mmm," Becca agreed.

"I guess you're really excited about Kwanzaa," Mallory continued.

Becca nodded silently, chewing on some bacon.

This was ridiculous. Mallory sighed and looked around. "Well, I guess I'll be hanging out in the living room, if you need me."

As she stood up, she noticed two big cardboard boxes in a corner of the dining room, one opened and one closed. The opened one had contained the Christmas tree decorations we'd used. The other was marked HOLIDAY/HOUSE DECORATIONS.

"Becca?" Mallory said. "Did you guys finish putting up your holiday decorations?"

"No," Becca called out.

"Do you want to?"

Becca peeked out into the dining room. "But it's after Christmas."

"So? Don't you want the house to look nice when your family comes home?"

A smile slowly worked its way across Becca's face. "Can I wear my Christmas dress, too?"

"Sure!"

As Becca bounced upstairs, Mallory began unloading the box. She took out two strings of indoor lights and began taping them around the front windows.

She was almost finished by the time Becca came down in her red-and-green velvet dress. She had pulled her hair back with a black satin ribbon, and she was wearing black patent leather shoes.

"Who-o-o-oa!" Mallory said. "Christmasy!"

"Kwanzaa-y," Becca corrected her. "And we have to replace some of those lights. Only keep red and green. The official Kwanzaa colors are red, black, and green. And there are no such things as *black* lights."

Becca and Mal pulled replacement lights out of the cardboard box. They were able to make only one string with red and green lights, so the lights didn't go all the way around the window. (It looked a little weird, but no one cared.)

The box was full of stuff that hadn't been touched for a year, such as a stained-glass Santa-with-reindeer we'd made the Christmas before, and a plastic snowman. Both of them were hung right on our front windows.

Mallory found a bag of pinecones and arranged them on our mantelpiece. Becca opened an old bag of tinsel and flung it onto the tree. Mallory frosted the windows with "snow" spray paint. Becca distributed little elf figurines around the living room.

Finally, from the bottom of the box, Becca pulled something wrapped in newspaper. As she ripped the paper off, she cried, "Ooooh, here's our *kinara* — and some candles!"

During the crazy week, we'd never found

our wooden Kwanzaa candleholder. Becca made sure to display it prominently on the mantel. "Daddy and Mama will be sooo surprised."

"I'll get a match," Mallory said.

"No!" Becca protested. "I want the whole family to light it. Besides, we have one more thing to do."

"What's that?"

Becca darted away to the family room and returned with some oaktag and a box of markers. "A sign for Squirt!"

They laid the oaktag on the dining room table and quickly drew this sign:

We arrived just as they were taping the sign to the front door.

I had the honor of carrying Squirt inside, but he was feeling tired and cranky. "Here he is!" I announced.

"Hi! Hi! Hi!" Becca shouted.

"WAAAAAAAAHH!" cried Squirt.

"He needs a nap," Mama said wearily.

"I need a nap," Daddy added.

"Rebecca, adjust the bow on your dress," Aunt Cecelia commanded.

We all walked right past the sign, through the house, and into the coat alcove by the kitchen. None of us said a word about the decorations. (Squirt had been a real handful, and we were exhausted.)

Mallory could see Becca's face fall.

"WAAAAAAH!" Squirt screamed as I took off his jacket.

Mallory and Becca followed me into the kitchen. "He sounds hungry," Mallory said. "I'll feed him."

As I hung up Squirt's jacket, Mallory opened a cupboard. Becca snatched up Squirt and smothered him with kisses.

"WAAAAAAAAHHH!"

"Rebecca, stop that!" Aunt Cecelia said. "You have the flu!"

"Ease up, Cecelia," Daddy said. "She can't still be contagious."

"Oh?" Aunt Cecelia replied. "And why, pray tell, do you suppose the doctor did not allow her into the hospital?"

"She's right, John," Mama said.

Mallory cut up a banana and poured a cupful of apple juice. As she brought it to the table, Becca was trying to get Squirt settled in his high chair. He was kicking so hard, his legs were like little pistons. Becca kept lifting and lowering his body, trying to aim his legs into the proper place. "Come on," she said.

"Careful!" Aunt Cecelia warned her. "He has had a head injury! We are supposed to be vigilant and gentle."

"She is being gentle," Mama insisted.

"He is not a jack-in-the-box," Aunt Cecelia said.

"*Cecelia, will you knock it off?*" Daddy thundered. "You haven't stopped grousing since we left the hospital. This is supposed to be a happy day — "

"And this is how you express your happiness?" Aunt Cecelia asked. "By yelling at your own sister in front of the children?"

Mama took Aunt Cecelia by the arm. "Kids, excuse us, please."

The grown-ups marched out of the kitchen.

I tried to feed Squirt his banana.

"*No! No! No!*" he shrieked.

"He's tired," Mallory said.

"He's confused," I guessed.

Becca gave me a pouty look. "You guys didn't even say anything about our decorations."

"I'm sorry," I said. "I'll look now."

As I ran toward the living room, Mallory

put her arm around Becca. "Give them a chance to settle down."

"Some first day of Kwanzaa," Becca muttered. "Remember what the theme is? *Umoja.* Togetherness."

"I will *not* apologize!" Daddy's voice boomed.

*"No-o-o-o-o-o-o!"* Squirt swept his arm across his tray, knocking the bananas to the floor. His apple juice went flying against the wall.

Mallory grabbed a sponge. Becca stomped off toward her bedroom.

Hoo boy.

Some *umoja.*

# CHAPTER 13

"*Habari gana?*" asked my uncle Charles.

He held a lit match to our *kinara*, and the second green candle from the end burst into flame.

Daddy looked at Mama. Aunt Cecelia tucked her napkin under her chin. Keisha and I exchanged a glance. Becca started giggling. Squirt flung peas at Kara Ramsey. Billy Ramsey reached over to tickle Squirt. (Billy is five and Kara's two. They are Keisha's siblings and my cousins.)

"Well?" Aunt Yvonne said. "Doesn't anybody remember?"

*Habari gana* is Swahili for "What is the news?" Someone is supposed to say it at the beginning of each night's Kwanzaa festivities.

Then everyone is supposed to give the answer: the theme for that day.

The trouble was, everyone had forgotten except Uncle Charles and Aunt Yvonne.

"Uh, which day of Kwanzaa is it?" Becca asked.

Uncle Charles smiled and counted slowly: "One, two, three, four . . . "

"Five!" Becca said. "That's . . . that's . . . "

"*Nia!*" Keisha said.

"Porpoise!" Billy blurted out.

I cracked up.

"Ehhhhh . . . ehhhhh . . . " Keisha bleated like Flipper.

"Keisha, please!" Aunt Cecelia said. "Behave."

(Yes, she acts like that with everyone.)

Keisha's family had arrived just in time for Monday dinner. They were rested and thrilled to see us. Boy, did they change the glum spirit in our house.

How did it feel to see so much happiness? Weird. Our lives had been kind of cheer-challenged for a long time.

Uncle Charles laughed at Keisha's imitation. "Well, at least he tried. It's *purpose*, Billy. Tonight we talk about what we plan to do in the year ahead."

Sleep.

Buy Aunt Cecelia a new ankle so she wouldn't complain so much.

Make a time machine so I could go back to December 15 and leave Squirt's belt buckled.

Invent a volume control that would shut out my dad's arguments with my aunt.

Turn life into a ballet so at least I could have a little fun.

Those were all the things I wanted to say. What a strange holiday season it had been. I'd thought things would improve after Squirt came home and Becca recovered. I mean, it was December 30, two days away from the new year and the Kwanzaa festival. And Keisha's family was visiting for three whole days!

I should have been happy. Was I? No way.

I felt as if we'd been fighting the holidays instead of enjoying them.

What had our Kwanzaa been like?

Well, first let me tell you how Kwanzaa is supposed to be.

Each night the festivities start with a candle lighting. The *kinara* holds seven candles, one for each day of Kwanzaa. The black candle in the middle is the longest, and it is always lit on the first night. The three smaller candles to the left are red, and they remind us of the struggles African-Americans have had to face. The three to the right are green, and they represent hope for a prosperous future.

On the second night, you light the red candle next to the middle one. Then, day by day, you alternate lighting green and red candles until the whole *kinara* is ablaze.

Kwanzaa is a family holiday. Each day's festivity usually starts whenever the family can come together (usually it's at dinnertime).

After someone asks *"Habari gana?"* you talk about the day's theme. Then you do an activity based on that.

The first day is easy. For *umoja*, togetherness, you just do family activities.

We did that, all right. We argued together about why Squirt was cranky. We worried together that he might black out again. We fought together about who was supposed to make dinner and clean up the Christmas garbage. We collapsed into our beds at the same time.

Day Two is *kujichagulia*, or self-determination. That's when you learn new African traditions or enjoy ones you already know — braiding hair, playing African musical instruments, dancing.

Squirt caught a traditional cold that day. He made traditional war cries from dawn to dusk. And we practiced our two newest Ramsey traditions: worrying and bickering.

On the third day (*ujima*, or collective work and responsibility), you're supposed to do a big family chore.

Aunt Cecelia must have misunderstood. She *was* a family chore. After an argument with Mama and Daddy, she stormed out of the house, yelling, "That's it! I am going for good. You can reach me at the Stamford YWCA!"

(Don't worry. She came back forty-five minutes later.)

I was really looking forward to the fourth day. The theme is kind of boring: cooperative economics, or *ujamaa*. But we actually had a fun theme activity planned. Since Keisha's family was arriving the next day, we had to do some shopping. (Get it? Shopping . . . economics?)

Daddy took in the mail just as we were about to leave. In it was a bill from the hospital. A huge bill. When Daddy read it, his jaw nearly made a dent in the floor.

*Whoosh.* Off to the phone. Daddy was able to use all the arguing skills he had practiced that week.

We left an hour later. Daddy said we had a "possible insurance limitation problem." I had no idea what that meant. But I noticed Mama crossing a lot of things off our shopping list before we started. And we had to buy store brands for every little thing.

I guess Becca and I were lucky. We actually escaped the house on Saturday and Sunday afternoons, for Kwanzaa festival meetings.

The festival was about the only thing going well in my life. *Malindy* was coming along. The kids had made more delicious food and some nice-looking crafts.

I couldn't wait to see Keisha's family. But you know what? Seeing them so happy and carefree made me depressed. All I could think was, why couldn't we have been like them? We had wasted the whole month being gloomy.

Oh, well, back to the dinner table.

"So," Uncle Charles said, "any ideas? How do we fill the days and years ahead?"

Aunt Cecelia looked straight at Daddy and said, "I believe some of us could use a little patience."

Daddy nearly choked on his turkey. "Well, gaining common sense might be a good thing for certain people," he retorted.

"John, please," Mama said.

"Not to mention remembering to side with one's spouse," Daddy snapped.

"Ummm..." Uncle Charles shot Aunt Yvonne a nervous look. "I was thinking about, you know, spending more family time together..."

"Teaching children to respect limits," Aunt Cecelia commented.

"Working in the community..." Uncle Charles pressed on.

119

"Learning to drive safely *through* the community," Daddy murmured.

Aunt Cecelia lifted her napkin from her lap and tossed it on the plate. "I have had enough. I believe I will excuse myself — "

Aunt Yvonne stood up. "Uh, listen, everybody. Maybe it wasn't such a great idea for us to visit. This is a tough time for you, and you certainly don't need the pressure of guests — "

"It's *okay*, Yvonne!" Daddy said. "Please sit down!"

"John Ramsey, they are not our *pets*!" Aunt Cecelia snapped. "When are you going to learn to talk *with* people, not at them? Look at the harm you've already done to the family."

"*I've* done?" Daddy retorted.

Squirt looked up from his mashed sweet potatoes with a start. His face crumbled and he exploded into tears.

Mama reached over to pick him up.

"Oh, you poor thing," Aunt Cecelia said. "How can you be expected to recover with all this thoughtless behavior — "

"Maybe we can visit at the end of January," Uncle Charles was saying.

"Don't be ridiculous," Daddy replied.

"Really — "

"Another day — "

"I won't hear of it — "

"Why don't we have some coffee?"

Mama, Daddy, Aunt Cecelia, Uncle Charles, and Aunt Yvonne were standing now, all talking at once. Squirt had buried his face in Mama's shoulder.

Keisha pressed her hands to her ears. "Sto-o-o-op!" she screamed.

The voices stopped. All the grown-ups spun to look at Keisha, as if she'd been hurt.

"Why are you fighting?" Keisha demanded. "This is so stupid! It's Kwanzaa. We need to celebrate!"

Squirt pulled his head back from Mama's shirt. He looked around, his eyes wide.

Then he smiled, pointed to Daddy, and burped.

Becca tried to swallow a laugh. It came out like a snort.

That made Billy laugh. Squirt started applauding himself and shouted "Bup! Bup!"

"Good one, Squirt!" Uncle Charles said.

"Yeaaaa!" all us kids shouted.

"Yeaaa bup!" Squirt said.

Aunt Cecelia was trying desperately not to smile. She shook her head and said, "You're only rewarding him . . . "

And then she cracked up. Yes, Aunt Cecelia. She was hooting and snickering. She had to grab the edge of the table to keep from falling over.

Daddy chuckled. He took one look at Mama,

who let out such a sudden laugh that a piece of collard green flew from her mouth and across the table.

That did it. We were all hysterical.

Daddy put his arm around Uncle Charles's shoulder. "I'm sorry, little brother. You, too, Cecelia."

"No, no, it's my fault!" Aunt Cecelia replied.

Uncle Charles was laughing so hard he had to catch his breath. "I say, you two, be quiet and let's all dig in!"

We did, too.

I hadn't tasted such a good dinner in a long time.

# CHAPTER 14

"What do you mean, 'It's yummy'?" Aunt Cecelia asked.

Keisha held out a bowl and I ladled some Hoppin' John into it. "Don't knock it until you've tried it, Aunt Cecelia," I said.

"Young ladies, I grew up with Hoppin' John," Aunt Cecelia replied. "I used to try to serve it to you both, back in Oakley, but you wouldn't eat it."

"Oops," said Keisha.

I handed Aunt Cecelia the bowl. "Kids change."

Aunt Cecelia took a spoonful and chewed slowly.

Around us, the Stoneybrook Community Center gym was filling up. Yes, the festival — my very own great idea — was underway. It was the perfect day for it, too: the theme for Kwanzaa's sixth day is *kuumba*, or creativity.

The sun was shining and it was New Year's Eve.

We'd opened the doors at noon, and the place had begun filling up right away. I recognized some African-American families from Stoneybrook — the Battses, Fords, Harrises, Ingrams, Hickses, and Olatunjis — but there were some faces I'd never seen before. ("Because of the fliers I put up in the other towns," Kristy said.)

Plenty of non-African-American families had stopped by, too. I overheard Buddy Barrett trying to convince his parents to celebrate Kwanzaa in their house. Timmy Hsu and Bob Ingram were leading a parade, waving the red-green-and-black *bendera ya taifa* flag. Jake Kuhn asked me why we were selling menorahs. (I had to explain they were *kinaras*.)

Of course, the entire BSC was on hand. Stacey was the festival's cashier. We had decided to donate our proceeds to a special fund for children's services at the Stoneybrook Hospital. (That was my idea.) Abby was the official stage manager for the show. Kristy was at the door, greeting families and handing out a guide to the festival (with a BSC flier tucked into it, of course).

Claudia had designed the guide. It was called "The Official Map and Guide to the First Annual Stoneybrook Kwanzaa Festival." It briefly explained the event, listed the participants, displayed the starting time for the play (2:00), and showed our arrangement of the gym.

Food was on tables against one wall, crafts against another. Posters were everywhere. The biggest one was an illustrated history and explanation of Kwanzaa. But my favorite art project was the mural of African-American portraits. Looking down at us were Frederick Douglass, Harriet Tubman, Marcus Garvey, Thurgood Marshall, Rosa Parks, Malcolm X, Shirley Chisholm, and Martin Luther King.

I felt in good hands.

At the far end, the stage was set for our play. We'd painted a rural backdrop, using Mary Anne's house as a model for the farmhouse. Claudia had done most of the sketching, but the kids had painted it. The farmhouse windows were pink, the sky had an orange-soda stain on it, and one of the chickens was saying "Duane Rules" in a speech bubble, but it looked great anyway.

Aunt Cecelia swallowed her Hoppin' John and said, "Needs thyme."

"We cooked it for hours!" I protested.

"Thyme, the spice," Aunt Cecelia explained. "And some cayenne pepper, too."

"Jessi!" Becca rushed up from behind me. "Jessi, I lost it!"

"Lost what?" I asked.

*"My script!"*

Becca was the narrator of *Malindy*. It was the only role I could give her. She had missed so many rehearsals, and the narrator doesn't need to memorize lines or act. "When we left home," I said, "it was in your backpack."

"It was? I'll check." Becca zoomed away.

"Uh, Jessi?" Keisha said. "Do you know that kid?"

I followed Keisha's glance to the beverage table. Marnie Barrett, a two-year-old BSC charge, was reaching up over her head for a very full cup of Caribbean fruit punch.

Yikes. I sprinted to the table and carried Marnie back to her family.

"Jessi!" Abby called from across the room. "Fifteen minutes to curtain! Spread the word!"

My stomach clenched up. The play was the only thing I was nervous about.

Mallory and I ran around, gathering up our actors. They headed backstage, which was a corner we'd roped off with a hanging sheet.

By the side of the stage, Rosie Wilder set up a music stand and took out her violin.

Boy, were the kids nervous. They couldn't stop yakking. They also couldn't seem to put on their costumes. Bob's finger caught in the zipper of his dog outfit (brown feet pajamas painted with white spots). Omar's plastic devil horns kept drooping. Duane's pig snout hurt his nose. Tomika popped a button on her plaid dress.

"Rosie!" Abby called out. "Start playing!"

As we frantically helped the kids, we could hear Rosie's version of "Turkey in the Straw."

Nine times.

Finally I stepped in front of the crowd, and Rosie stopped.

"Welcome to the Stoneybrook Kwanzaa Festival's production of *Malindy and Little Devil!*" I announced.

The whole room cheered and whistled.

From the front row I heard Kristy whisper, "Mention the Baby-sitters Club!"

"This play is based on a traditional African-American folktale from the South," I continued, "traced back to the late nineteenth century. The kids you're about to see have worked very hard. I'd like to thank them, and also the members of the Baby-sitters Club for their help — "

Kristy stood up. "Our number is on the flier!"

"And now," I shouted, before Kristy could say another word, "I present your narrator, Becca Ramsey!"

I turned. Abby had folded back the black drape, and Becca was standing there.

Frozen.

She was gazing at me as if she were headed for the gallows.

"Go ahead," I said.

"I — " Becca's voice caught in her throat. "I — "

"Somebody go!" Abby urged.

Bob darted around Becca and sprang onto the stage. "Roof! Roof!" he barked.

"Beeeaaaaahh!" bleated Ebon, crawling onto the platform after Bob.

Out walked Duane the pig. "Oiiiiink!" he squealed in Bob's ear.

"RAAWWWWWF!" Bob howled, pushing Duane to the floor with his hand.

*"BEEEEEEEAAAAH!"* Ebon butted Bob's chest.

"Oh, no," Abby moaned. "They're getting carried away!"

I could hear a few puzzled laughs in the audience. "Becca," I whispered. "We need your help."

Becca unlocked her knees and stepped timidly onto the platform. "Um . . . " She held the script in front of her face. "Once-upon-a-time-there-was-a-little-girl-named-Malindy-who-lived-on-a-farm."

The animals fell suddenly silent. Becca looked over the top of her script, startled. Then she smiled.

Aunt Cecelia started clapping. Then Daddy

and Mama. In a moment, the whole crowd had joined in.

"They *like* me!" Bob exclaimed. He stood up and took a bow, but I don't think Becca noticed. She was grinning up a storm.

"Well, Malindy just *loooooooved* to sing and dance," Becca proclaimed loudly. "Hey, yo, here she comes now!"

"That's not in the script," Abby whispered to me.

"What a ham," I said.

Sharelle skipped out onto the stage with a bucket full of shredded white paper. "I'm going to get some milk from the moo cow!" she sang.

Our cow was Laurel and Patsy Kuhn, covered with a brown sheet (Laurel was the front part, and she held a papier-mâché cow mask).

As Sharelle pretended to milk the cow (the udders were a surgeon's glove filled with air), Omar sneaked onto the stage. Clutching his rubber pitchfork, he sneered at the audience and said, "Nyah-hah-hah!"

"Sssssss!" some people hissed.

"Booo!" cried a few others.

Omar looked crushed.

"That's what they're supposed to do!" Abby whispered from behind him. "It means you're doing well!"

Sharelle stood up and began skipping in

Omar's direction. Then she dropped her bucket and screamed, "EEEEEK!"

The shredded paper was stuck inside. Duane pounced on it and began throwing the shreds out. "It's supposed to be milk," he explained to the audience.

Well, Omar told her he'd restore her milk for a price — her soul. And Sharelle said she wanted to live a long, long life. Say, to ten years old or so. So Omar agreed to wait. The years went by (and all the kids had a chance to play minor parts). Malindy became Sara, then Tomika.

At the big climax, Tomika gave Omar the sole of a shoe.

"That's it?" Omar said. "I thought it was bigger."

Tomika shrugged. "That's all. Now get out of here before I whup your tail."

She pretend-kicked him, and Omar scurried offstage.

"And Malindy lived happily ever after," Becca announced. "Because the devil can only get your soul once, and then he has to stop. The end."

Daddy shot to his feet. "Bravo!"

Guess what? We had an instant standing ovation.

"And here are the writers!" Becca shouted. "Mallory Pike and my sister, Jessi Ramsey."

We stood on the stage and bowed — Mallory, Abby, and the whole cast.

After the play, we were mobbed. Our friends in the BSC lifted Mallory and me off the ground and led a "Two, four, six, eight" cheer. Keisha promised to help me run the festival next year. I took Squirt from Mama and he couldn't stop hugging me. People I didn't know were shouting, "Great job!"

Aunt Cecelia gave me a big kiss. "I was so proud of you both," she whispered. (I may be wrong, but I think her mascara was running.)

As for Becca, well, I saw her signing autographs for two admiring little boys.

I was flying. I hadn't felt so good in weeks.

As people started moseying back to the displays, Mallory put her arm around my shoulders. "We did it."

"We sure did!" I gave her a big, long squeeze. "Thanks for coming through, Mallory!"

Mal smiled. "Are you hungry? I'm starving."

I took her arm, and we headed toward the food table.

Parts of the play were running in my mind, especially the mistakes. And a few unexpected lines.

"I could not believe it when Omar looked at the sole and said, 'Ew, you shouldn't have walked in the cow shed'!" I said to Mallory.

Mallory laughed. "I think Abby taught him that."

"That was my favorite part."

"Nahh, not mine."

I turned to face her. She was beaming. "My favorite part is right now," she explained. "Seeing Jessi Ramsey finally back to her old self."

I wasn't expecting her to say that.

But you know what?

I had to agree.

# CHAPTER 15

"*Harambee! Harambee! Harambee! Harambee! Harambee! Harambee!*"

I love that word. It's Swahili for "Let's all pull together," and you're supposed to call it out once on the first day of Kwanzaa, twice on the second, and so on. But I just love the way it sounds. If the word were something like "Farquar" or "Ziziphus," it just wouldn't be as much fun to shout.

And all of us — Mama, Daddy, Becca, Keisha, Billy, Aunt Yvonne, Uncle Charles, Aunt Cecelia, and I — were shouting it as loudly as we could. (Kara shouted, "Hambee!" and Squirt just sucked his thumb.)

On New Year's Eve, just a few hours after the Kwanzaa festival was over, us Ramseys held our *karamu*.

*Karamu* is one of the best parts of Kwanzaa. It's a fancy feast and a ceremony. Mama was dressed in a long, flowing *busuti*, a robe tied with a sash at the waist. Aunt Yvonne wore a green-and-red *buba*, a loose-fitting gown. She'd wrapped her hair in a matching cloth called a *gele*, and she looked like a queen. Daddy and Uncle Charles were both wearing *dashikis*, which are long, brightly colored shirts.

Daddy spread our fancy *mkeke* mat on the dining room table. "No matter how high a house is built," he said, "it must stand on something."

That's a traditional Kwanzaa statement. And boy, is it true.

"I think, over the last month," Mama said, "we all learned how strong a foundation the Ramsey family stands on."

Aunt Cecelia nodded. "Amen."

Uncle Charles and Aunt Yvonne set bowls of fruit on the table, plus a couple of ears of corn. These are symbols of the harvest.

Standing at the head of the table, Daddy raised a big pewter goblet full of water. We use the goblet only once a year. It's the *kikombe cha umoja*, or "unity cup."

Daddy carefully held up the cup to face the north, south, east, and west winds. Then he tipped the cup toward the floor. "We spill a few drops to honor our ancestors."

As the water tumbled to the carpet, Becca said, "Ooooh, who's going to clean that?"

Aunt Cecelia chuckled. "Don't look at me."

"Ahem," Daddy said. "And now we pass the cup around."

Aunt Yvonne took it and made a sipping gesture.

"Ewwww," Billy said. "We have to share germs?"

"You just pretend," Keisha whispered.

Mama was the last to take the cup. She stood up and said, "This year I am supposed to give the *kukaribisha*, the opening speech of our little family ceremony. Last night I tried and tried to write down something to say. I thought about today's theme: creativity. And I looked ahead to tomorrow's: faith. And somehow, when I thought of those two words, I kept seeing the faces of my beautiful daughters."

Mama smiled at me and Becca, and I felt like dancing.

"We saw their creativity at the wonderful festival today," Mama went on. "But it was their faith that pulled this family through a trying time — faith that their brother would be all right, faith that the Ramseys would be unified, faith that the festival could be organized despite all our setbacks. So, Becca and Jessi, if you're up to it, I'd like to give you both the honor of saying this year's *kukaribisha*."

Huh?

I sure wasn't expecting that. I thought *her* speech was just fine by itself.

Becca stood up, edged away from her chair, and said, "Uh, I have to go to the bathroom."

Whoosh. She was history.

Now everyone was looking at me.

"Go for it," Keisha said.

I rose to my feet. My mind was a jumble. "Uh . . . well . . . " I began.

As I looked around the room, I spotted the big Kwanzaa poster we had made for the festival. I'd brought it home and propped it against the wall. On it was the farewell statement that had been written for the *karamu* by the creator of Kwanzaa, Dr. Karenga.

"I'm not supposed to say this until the end of dinner," I said, "but it fits right now." I read loudly and clearly: " 'May the year's end meet us laughing and stronger.' "

"That's right!" Uncle Charles proclaimed.

In the candlelight of the *kinara*, Mama and Daddy seemed to be shining from within. Aunt Yvonne and Uncle Charles looked relaxed and happy. Squirt and Kara were shoveling bananas into their mouths, and Keisha and Billy were all smiles. Even Aunt Cecelia looked calm and content.

"And one more thing," I added. "May we all

be here at this table again next year, as happy and healthy as we are now!"

*"Harambee!"* Becca's voice rang out from the bathroom.

*"HAAAARAAAMMBEEEEEE!"* shouted the rest of the Ramsey family.

I think they could have heard us in the next town.

Dear Reader,

In *Happy Holidays, Jessi*, the Ramseys face a trying time, but in the end the strength of their family and of family traditions pulls them through. When I was growing up, one of our holiday traditions involved our neighbors, the Rices. We were very close to them, and the Rice kids were my first baby-sitting charges. Starting when I was young, our families got together every single year at Christmastime to exchange gifts and celebrate the holiday. On most years we got together on Christmas Eve. We usually had dinner at a restaurant called Good Time Charley's, and then gathered at either their house or ours to exchange presents. Now many years have passed, and we've all gone through lots of changes. The Rice kids are married now, and Robert even has kids of his own. Everyone has scattered. We live all up and down the East Coast. But if we can, we still try to get together. It's an important tradition. Families, friends, togetherness — that's what holidays are all about.

Happy holidays!

*Ann M Martin*

L. GODWIN

# Ann M. Martin

# About the Author

ANN MATTHEWS MARTIN was born on August 12, 1955. She grew up in Princeton, NJ, with her parents and her younger sister, Jane.

Although Ann used to be a teacher and then an editor of children's books, she's now a full-time writer. She gets the ideas for her books from many different places. Some are based on personal experiences. Others are based on childhood memories and feelings. Many are written about contemporary problems or events.

All of Ann's characters, even the members of the Baby-sitters Club, are made up. (So is Stoneybrook.) But many of her characters are based on real people. Sometimes Ann names her characters after people she knows, other times she chooses names she likes.

In addition to the Baby-sitters Club books, Ann Martin has written many other books for children. Her favorite is *Ten Kids, No Pets* because she loves big families and she loves animals. Her favorite Baby-sitters Club book is *Kristy's Big Day*. (By the way, Kristy is her favorite baby-sitter!)

Ann M. Martin now lives in New York with her cats, Gussie and Woody. Her hobbies are reading, sewing, and needlework — especially making clothes for children.

# Notebook Pages

This Baby-sitters Club book belongs to _____.

I am _____ years old and in the _____

grade.

The name of my school is _____

I got this BSC book from _____

I started reading it on _____ and

finished reading it on _____

The place where I read most of this book is _____.

My favorite part was when _____.

If I could change anything in the story, it might be the part when

_____

My favorite character in the Baby-sitters Club is _____

The BSC member I am most like is _____

because _____

If I could write a Baby-sitters Club book it would be about _____

_____

# #103 Happy Holidays, Jessi

Kwaanza is one of Jessi's favorite holidays. My favorite holiday

is _____ because _____

_____

_____ . On this holiday, my family usually

_____

_____ . If I could spend this

holiday with anybody in the world, I would spend it with _____

_____ . If I were making my own

holiday, I would call it _____

_____ and it would happen in the month of _____

_____ . This is how we would celebrate

my holiday: _____

_____

_____ . Some holidays have symbols — like a Kinara

for Kwaanza, a tree for Christmas, or a Menorah for Hanukkah.

The symbol for my holiday would look like this:

# JESSI'S

This is me at age four.

Me with my new baby brother.

I'm always happy when I'm dancing.

# SCRAPBOOK

*Matt and Haley Braddock, two of my favorite charges.*

*My family—Daddy and Mama Becca, me, Aunt Cecelia and Squirt.*

Read all the books
about **Jessi**
in the Baby-sitters Club series
by Ann M. Martin

# THE BABY-SITTERS Club

Look for #104

## ABBY'S TWIN

The same but different. That's Anna and me exactly. We look alike, yet we don't dress alike or wear our hair alike. Our personalities are different, but sometimes we are the same in the most strange ways. (We both like the same movies almost all the time, for example. Once we both bought my mother the exact same pair of earrings for her birthday without even discussing it. Things like that.)

And now, apparently, we were the same in a new way. We both had scoliosis.

I looked up at Anna, standing by the coffee table. Strangely enough, I realized I was almost glad she'd gotten a note, too. It made me feel less alone.

She must have been feeling the same thing, because she said, "We'll get through it together, Abby. Don't worry."

I forced a little smile. "Okay, twin," I said. "You're right. We'll get through it together."

# THE BABY-SITTERS CLUB®

**Collect 'em all!**

## 100 (and more)
## Reasons to Stay Friends Forever!

*More titles...* ➧

### The Baby-sitters Club titles continued...

| | | | |
|---|---|---|---|
| ❑ MG48226-2 | #82 | Jessi and the Troublemaker | $3.99 |
| ❑ MG48235-1 | #83 | Stacey vs. the BSC | $3.50 |
| ❑ MG48228-9 | #84 | Dawn and the School Spirit War | $3.50 |
| ❑ MG48236-X | #85 | Claudi Kishi, Live from WSTO | $3.50 |
| ❑ MG48227-0 | #86 | Mary Anne and Camp BSC | $3.50 |
| ❑ MG48237-8 | #87 | Stacey and the Bad Girls | $3.50 |
| ❑ MG22872-2 | #88 | Farewell, Dawn | $3.50 |
| ❑ MG22873-0 | #89 | Kristy and the Dirty Diapers | $3.50 |
| ❑ MG22874-9 | #90 | Welcome to the BSC, Abby | $3.99 |
| ❑ MG22875-1 | #91 | Claudia and the First Thanksgiving | $3.50 |
| ❑ MG22876-5 | #92 | Mallory's Christmas Wish | $3.50 |
| ❑ MG22877-3 | #93 | Mary Anne and the Memory Garden | $3.99 |
| ❑ MG22878-1 | #94 | Stacey McGill, Super Sitter | $3.99 |
| ❑ MG22879-X | #95 | Kristy + Bart = ? | $3.99 |
| ❑ MG22880-3 | #96 | Abby's Lucky Thirteen | $3.99 |
| ❑ MG22881-1 | #97 | Claudia and the World's Cutest Baby | $3.99 |
| ❑ MG22882-X | #98 | Dawn and Too Many Sitters | $3.99 |
| ❑ MG69205-4 | #99 | Stacey's Broken Heart | $3.99 |
| ❑ MG69206-2 | #100 | Kristy's Worst Idea | $3.99 |
| ❑ MG69207-0 | #101 | Claudia Kishi, Middle School Dropout | $3.99 |
| ❑ MG69208-9 | #102 | Mary Anne and the Little Princess | $3.99 |
| ❑ MG69209-7 | #103 | Happy Holidays, Jessi | $3.99 |
| ❑ MG45575-3 | | Logan's Story Special Edition Readers' Request | $3.25 |
| ❑ MG47118-X | | Logan Bruno, Boy Baby-sitter Special Edition Readers' Request | $3.50 |
| ❑ MG47756-0 | | Shannon's Story Special Edition | $3.50 |
| ❑ MG47686-6 | | The Baby-sitters Club Guide to Baby-sitting | $3.25 |
| ❑ MG47314-X | | The Baby-sitters Club Trivia and Puzzle Fun Book | $2.50 |
| ❑ MG48400-1 | | BSC Portrait Collection: Claudia's Book | $3.50 |
| ❑ MG22864-1 | | BSC Portrait Collection: Dawn's Book | $3.50 |
| ❑ MG69181-3 | | BSC Portrait Collection: Kristy's Book | $3.99 |
| ❑ MG22865-X | | BSC Portrait Collection: Mary Anne's Book | $3.99 |
| ❑ MG48399-4 | | BSC Portrait Collection: Stacey's Book | $3.50 |
| ❑ MG92713-2 | | The Complete Guide to The Baby-sitters Club | $4.95 |
| ❑ MG47151-1 | | The Baby-sitters Club Chain Letter | $14.95 |
| ❑ MG48295-5 | | The Baby-sitters Club Secret Santa | $14.95 |
| ❑ MG45074-3 | | The Baby-sitters Club Notebook | $2.50 |
| ❑ MG44783-1 | | The Baby-sitters Club Postcard Book | $4.95 |

**Available wherever you buy books...or use this order form.**
Scholastic Inc., P.O. Box 7502, 2931 E. McCarty Street, Jefferson City, MO 65102

Please send me the books I have checked above. I am enclosing $_____
(please add $2.00 to cover shipping and handling). Send check or money order–
no cash or C.O.D.s please.

Name_____ Birthdate_____

Address _____

City_____ State/Zip_____

BSC5962

# THE BABY-SITTERS CLUB®

## by Ann M. Martin

## Collect and read these exciting BSC Super Specials, Mysteries, and Super Mysteries along with your favorite Baby-sitters Club books!

### BSC Super Specials

| | | | |
|---|---|---|---|
| ❑ | BBK44240-6 | Baby-sitters on Board! Super Special #1 | $3.95 |
| ❑ | BBK44239-2 | Baby-sitters' Summer Vacation  Super Special #2 | $3.95 |
| ❑ | BBK43973-1 | Baby-sitters' Winter Vacation  Super Special #3 | $3.95 |
| ❑ | BBK42493-9 | Baby-sitters' Island Adventure  Super Special #4 | $3.95 |
| ❑ | BBK43575-2 | California Girls! Super Special #5 | $3.95 |
| ❑ | BBK43576-0 | New York, New York! Super Special #6 | $4.50 |
| ❑ | BBK44963-X | Snowbound! Super Special #7 | $3.95 |
| ❑ | BBK44962-X | Baby-sitters at Shadow Lake  Super Special #8 | $3.95 |
| ❑ | BBK45661-X | Starring The Baby-sitters Club! Super Special #9 | $3.95 |
| ❑ | BBK45674-1 | Sea City, Here We Come! Super Special #10 | $3.95 |
| ❑ | BBK47015-9 | The Baby-sitters Remember  Super Special #11 | $3.95 |
| ❑ | BBK48308-0 | Here Come the Bridesmaids! Super Special #12 | $3.95 |
| ❑ | BBK22883-8 | Aloha, Baby-sitters! Super Special #13 | $4.50 |

### BSC Mysteries

| | | | |
|---|---|---|---|
| ❑ | BAI44084-5 | #1 Stacey and the Missing Ring | $3.50 |
| ❑ | BAI44085-3 | #2 Beware Dawn! | $3.50 |
| ❑ | BAI44799-8 | #3 Mallory and the Ghost Cat | $3.50 |
| ❑ | BAI44800-5 | #4 Kristy and the Missing Child | $3.50 |
| ❑ | BAI44801-3 | #5 Mary Anne and the Secret in the Attic | $3.50 |
| ❑ | BAI44961-3 | #6 The Mystery at Claudia's House | $3.50 |
| ❑ | BAI44960-5 | #7 Dawn and the Disappearing Dogs | $3.50 |
| ❑ | BAI44959-1 | #8 Jessi and the Jewel Thieves | $3.50 |
| ❑ | BAI44958-3 | #9 Kristy and the Haunted Mansion | $3.50 |
| ❑ | BAI45696-2 | #10 Stacey and the Mystery Money | $3.50 |

More titles ➡

## The Baby-sitters Club books continued...